Death and Taxis

an Al Pennyback mystery

Charles Ray

North Potomac, MD

This book is a work of fiction. Names, descriptions, places, and incidents are products of the author's imagination, or are used fictionally. Any resemblance to actual events or persons, living or dead, is purely coincidental.

The reproduction or distribution, by any means, including electronic distribution, is expressly prohibited without the written consent of the copyright holder, except for fair use quotes in connection with reviews.

For information about this and other works of this author, contact the author at charlesray.author@yahoo.com.

Printed in the United States of America.

Death and Taxis

One

"Al, I hate to bother you on a weekend, but I really need your help, bro."

Buster, that's my friend Detective Lieutenant Buster Mayweather of the District of Columbia Metropolitan Police Department, is not one to ask for help normally. In fact, it's usually me asking him for help.

But, here he was, sitting with me on my back porch just before noon on a Saturday in late November, with a hang dog look on his dark brown face. The weather had unexpectedly turned nice, with just a hint of chill in the breeze, so I was taking full advantage of it by having a late Saturday breakfast on the porch when he arrived.

At six-two, with two hundred twenty pounds of hard muscle that no amount of stopping at Dunkin Donuts has softened, Buster is an intimidating presence on the streets where he works gang activity. So, seeing him looking forlorn and frustrated was strange – strange and unsettling.

"No problem, amigo," I said. "After all, what are friends for? How can I help you?"

He hunched over in the chair, causing the wicker frame to creak loudly, and making me worry whether or not it was strong enough to hold him for long. Cupping the mug of hot cocoa Sandra had given him in his huge hands, his brow furrowed in concentration, he still managed to look intimidating. Whatever it was that was eating at him, though, he was having trouble spitting it out. I sat back and took a sip of my own cocoa – Sandra had made mine light on the sugar but heavy on the cream, just like I like it – and let him have the space he needed. While he struggled with whatever it was that was bugging him, I gazed at the stand of oak, maple, chestnut, sugar gum and beech trees behind the old farm house I call home. It seems like every year the trees get closer and closer to the house. I keep the grass cut, but that doesn't stop the deer from using my back yard as their favorite grazing place, or the squirrels that scamper to and fro scarping up nuts to stow away for the coming winter. I watched one squirrel in particular; in a huge old oak tree right at the edge of the tree line; zipping up and down the trunk building a nest in the crook of a limb about three-quarters the way to the top. He'd run down the side, and leap to a limb that still had green leaves on it, yank off a good size twig, and then scoot back up and stuff that into the growing ball of foliage in which he'd spend most of the winter. I imagine he – and I was just assuming the damn thing was male, and that his mate was out somewhere gathering nuts with which they'd line the bottom of the nest he was building – was looking forward to hunkering down when winter finally settled in, cuddling with his old lady and dreaming of the warmth of spring. When I got tired of looking at the squirrel, I focused on the leaves – the yellow, orange, brown, and gold, with splashes of green where a few stubborn leaves refused to turn and continued to cling to their branches. I'd find a particular large leaf that looked like it was ready to begin its spiraling journey to the mossy earth below, and watch it, almost willing it to fall. Sometimes I'd be rewarded with the sight of the leaf letting go and starting its downward journey – most times, I'd just stare at a leaf until my eyes felt like they would cross; at which time, I'd go back to watching the squirrel. He was making good progress on his nest, but kept adding small twigs here and there. Made me think that maybe *he* was a *she* – the males of the species, whether four-legged or two, aren't that in to the nuances of decoration.

Buster cleared his throat. He'd finally found the words.

"It's like this," he said. "There have been six murders in the city over the past two weeks."

"Sounds like you should be celebrating," I said. "That's a low number of homicides for D.C."

"Naw, that ain't what I mean. I mean, there have been six *particular* killings in the past two weeks – six cab drivers in different parts of town have been found with their taxis parked in alleys and their throats cut."

"Okay, I'll admit that's a different situation. But, how the hell is a private detective supposed to help a cop solve the murder of a few cab drivers?"

How, indeed! While Buster was a veteran detective – a one-time college football star who had blown his knees out, killing any chance he had of joining the NFL, and decided being a cop was the next best thing. I, on the other hand, was a retired army special ops type who had been convinced by a friend to get my PI license to make use of the dubious skills I'd picked up after twenty years of skulking around jungles, deserts, mountains, and villages of places I still can't talk about.

Buster and I had been friends, though, for over a decade. We'd met when my late wife, Sarah, and my son, Ethan, were killed, along with most of Ethan's soccer team, when a truck driver ran a stop sign coming onto Arlington Boulevard in Northern Virginia and T-boned the van Sarah was driving. It was Buster, then a detective first class on the DC force, who had come to my house in Georgetown with the two uniformed Arlington County cops to notify me of the accident and accompany me to the morgue to identify what was left of my family. He'd stayed with me afterwards when I came apart at the seams, quietly sitting there to let me know that I wasn't alone. We'd been friends since. He'd been there for me, so even though I had no idea how I could help him, if he needed me, I'd be there for him.

"I ain't got nowhere else to turn, bro," he said. "These cases are driving me nuts. You got a way of seeing through the bullshit, so I thought if I ran it past you; you might be able to help me figure out what's going on."

"Hey, Buster; if I can help you know I'll do my best. I'm just surprised – you've never been on the asking side before."

"That ain't true, and you know it. Remember that time them rednecks from West Virginia kidnapped Alma? I come to you for help then."

How well I remembered that episode. Buster and his wife Alma, pregnant at the time, had witnessed the murder of a militiaman by his comrades on a West Virginia country road, and the militia had kidnapped Alma to force him to be quiet about what he'd seen. That was a mistake – going after someone close to a friend of mine – and they compounded it by kidnapping Sandra Winter, my girlfriend, when they took Alma. Okay, so he had me. I'd helped him once. But, he'd helped me dozens of times.

"All right, I helped you once. But, what can I do for you now? You have the resources of the police department pretty much at your beck and call."

"Look, I know that, but right now, those resources are being diverted in some unproductive directions." The veins in his neck were knotted in frustration. I was afraid he'd crush the cup he was holding. "See, they got this new task force in the department – devoted to dealing with street crime. There's been a lot of muggings and assaults, some on tourists, on the Mall and in other upscale areas, and the mayor and city council have been making noise about it. Hurts revenue, you know. Anyhow, the chief formed this task force to deal with it, and they think these taxi driver killings are their jurisdiction – say they're just robberies turned violent. I say that's bullshit."

"So, what's wrong with their theory?" I asked. "Seems like if a task force is digging into it, they ought to solve it pretty soon – they can focus on it a lot better than a cop who has to handle a lot of other cases."

"Yeah, that would be the case," he said, making a snorting noise through his flared nostrils. "But, they're looking in all the wrong places. Besides, the task force chief is a real dickhead who wouldn't know a real clue if it walked up and kicked him in the balls. He's a captain who has been working community outreach and shit for the past ten years – no real experience doing police work on the streets. He's a total bureaucrat, and I can't get him to listen to me about this case."

"What is it you want him to hear, bro?"

"That, these killings ain't just ordinary street crime," he said. "Look, Al; two of the drivers that were killed just happen to be two of my CIs. I been working a network of informants looking at gang efforts to organize in the immigrant community. I'm hearing rumbling that somebody's tryin' to pull all the street gangs together under one leader, and if that happens it'll be hell trying to control gang activity. Having two of my confidential informants iced in such a short space of time can't be a coincidence."

I tended to agree with him about coincidence – I don't really believe in it. On the other hand, the number of violent deaths in D.C., or any other major city for that matter, is high, and two of six killings could just be random. My first inclination, despite his assessment of the head of the street crime task force, was that the man was right – these sounded to me like robberies that got out of hand. Happens all the time in the city.

"What makes you think they're not just random killings – or like the man says - robberies that got violent?"

"Mostly a gut feeling," he said. "But, my two guys happened to be from the immigrant community. One was a Nigerian who's been here for ten years, and the other was a recent arrival from Cameroon. They were reporting some good stuff about what's been happening in the community, and I think that's why they were killed. I was close to finding out who's behind this rumor of a gang merger."

"But, why cab drivers?"

Despite having been his friend for a long time, and working sometimes with, sometimes at cross purposes with, the police, the methods they used to select informants wasn't clear. I knew, for instance, that often the cops would use low level drug addicts or street pushers as CIs in their efforts to get the big fish, or small time thieves to get at the ring leaders; but, I couldn't see where taxicab drivers fit into any of that.

"A few months ago," Buster said. "We started picking up hints that someone was making a move to organize the gangs in the immigrant communities in the city, starting with the African, Caribbean and Central Americans first. Word was that whoever was behind it planned to bring all the criminal activity under one leader. Problem was, we didn't have a clue who was behind it. So, when I started looking into it, I ran across a few cab drivers who were pretty well tied into the community – one in particular is a kind of community leader who used to drive cabs, but now spends full time doing community outreach and stuff. I approached him, and after a few weeks, he agreed to work with me to keep it from happening, and talked a few of his fellow cabbies to go along. Man, you know how it is. Cab drivers are all over the place – they see everything, and can just about go anywhere without being noticed."

"I don't see how a guy driving a cab can give you much information about gang activity."

He laughed. It was a humorless, guttural sound. "That, my friend, is 'cause you never ride in cabs, and you don't know what goes on in the hood. Cab drivers go everywhere, know everyone, and see what goes down all the time. They know who meets who, and where and when they meet. Because they don't have criminal records – well, most of 'em don't - they're pretty much ignored. Makes 'em perfect informants, 'cause nobody gives 'em a second glance – until now. I think somebody's tumbled to it, and is tryin' to eliminate my sources of information. Makes me think I was close to whoever's runnin' this operation."

"But, your friend running the task force disagrees?"

"Yeah – that dipshit never agreed with me about usin' drivers as CIs in the first place. Dumbass don't know the drivers know who's runnin' numbers, who's dealin' drugs, the whole deal. Fact is, he don't know much 'bout good police work. Man's only good with press conferences and making good appearances."

As I thought over what he was saying, I could see his logic. "But, don't you have some arrests from the stuff they bring you to show they're worth the effort?"

"Uh, well . . . see . . . I haven't made any arrests." When I looked at him with a big question in my expression, he held up his hands defensively. "Look, bro, I'm after the big fish here. Bustin' some low level gang bangers ain't gonna do it – and, it could scare off whoever's behind the whole thing. I was gettin' a feelin' I was closin' in too, but now, with these guys gettin' iced, the drivers are gettin' nervous, and I can't get any of 'em to talk to me anymore 'cept for Joe, the community organizer."

"If you're right that these killings are really targeted at your informants, I can't say I blame them," I said. "Okay, what do you want me to do?"

"For starters, I want you to go to church with me tomorrow."

Now, I was looking at him in surprise. "And, just how is going to listen to some preacher threatening people with fire and brimstone supposed to help us find a killer?"

"Look, I know how you feel 'bout preachers, Al," he said. "You bein' a Buddhist and all. But, this ain't that kind of church – at least, I don't think it is. Mostly a bunch of African immigrants, and there'll be a bunch of cabbies there. It's the funeral for the Nigerian driver. I was kind of hopin' you'd be able to pick up some vibes that might help me get to the bottom of this mess."

Actually, my following Buddhist philosophy had nothing to do with my reluctance to go to church. I'd lost whatever religion my mother had tried to pound into me long before I left high school. I guess I'd just seen too many folk talk all high and holy on Sunday after doing some pretty raunchy stuff on Saturday. I'd seen these same folk leave church and then lie, cheat and steal for the rest of the week. It had pretty much turned me off of the whole organized religion thing. But, if Buster thought I might pick up on some clues by going to the cabbie's funeral, I could hold my nose and do it. That's what friendship is all about – doing things for a friend, even when they're unpleasant.

"Okay," I said. "I think I have a dark suit."

Death and Taxis

Two

Buster was back at my place at ten Sunday morning. Sandra and I had just finished a late Sunday breakfast, and I'd ironed the wrinkles out of the only dark suit I owned. Sandra watched in amusement as I struggled to knot a dark blue tie over a pearl grey shirt, the collar of which was about an eighth of an inch too tight. When it was apparent that I'd be there all morning getting the damned thing tied, she helped. Got it knotted perfectly with a few deft flips of her hand, adjusted it against my neck, and patted me on the cheek.

"Now, don't you look fine," he said as Sandra moved to the door to let him. "You look just like an old time preacher."

I ignored him, which brought chuckles from both him and Sandra.

"He's right, you know," she said.

"Hey," I said. "You're supposed to be on my side."

She kissed me on the cheek. "I am, babe – I am, but I've never seen you dressed up like this before. You look kind of cute." She brushed a finger against my cheek and batted her long lashes at me. The smell of the lavender soap she'd used to shower with made me want to rip the tie off and tell Buster to go to the funeral by himself.

But, you never break a promise to a friend.

"Yeah, and if you two keep this up, you'll never see me dressed like this again."

Buster clapped me on the shoulder. "Come on, bro. We got a funeral to go to."

We used his car; a 1999 Chevy Impala in metallic blue with a high performance engine that growled like a NASCAR racer as we bumped over the dirt lane leading from my farm house to River Road. Even with my seatbelt fastened, I gripped the arm rest tightly as he tore up through Potomac Village five miles per hour over the posted limit.

We stayed on River Road, across the I-495 Beltway, coming into the District from Montgomery County to Wisconsin Avenue just north of American University. A few blocks south on Wisconsin, we cut east on Ylima

Street over to Connecticut Avenue and turned south toward the National Zoo. We turned east on Calvert, crossing the Duke Ellington Memorial Bridge until Calvert became Euclid, and stayed on that street until we came to Sixteenth Street. We turned left on Sixteenth and went north to Mount Pleasant.

Abyssinian African Methodist Episcopal Church was a small, white clapboard building with a traditional bell tower and steeple set on a small grass covered knoll just off Monroe Street. The neighborhood was a collection of small red brick and wooden houses in various colors, with postage stamp lawns, bushy azaleas, and neatly trimmed shrubs, many with pickups or vans parked in front. The street in front of the church was lined on both sides with older model cars, pickups, vans, and SUVs. Mixed in among them were about a dozen cabs from the various hack companies that work in the District. A few people, mostly African from the colorful dresses and large posteriors on the women, walked in the brisk morning air. Directly in front of the church, a black hearse was parked. Buster found a parking spot about two blocks away and we walked back.

A few people gave us looks as we entered the church and took seats in the back pew. The looks weren't unfriendly, but they weren't particularly friendly either. We were outsiders, though, in a community that wasn't used to having outsiders around. Sitting in front of us were ten men, a few blacks, several swarthy men who looked like Indians or Pakistanis, and two elderly white guys – I assumed these were fellow cabbies come to pay their respects. The rest of the church was all African. At least, I assumed the throng of black people filling the pews was African because few of the African immigrants associated with the non-African blacks in the city – an avoidance that seemed to be mutual. Whoever thinks that sharing skin color meant people automatically associated with each other has only to visit one of the growing African immigrant communities in any major city like Washington. With their tribal and clan differences brought over from their home countries, many find it hard enough to get along with each other – and some never do. Many of the new arrivals find it impossible to find common ground with American blacks, who, despite calling themselves African-American, are all-American.

The place had that smell I remembered from childhood – talcum powder, sweat, cloying perfume, on body and from the flowers that surrounded the casket sitting on a bier just below the pulpit. There was a steady hum of quiet conversation as people waited for the preacher to put in an appearance. A cute young woman with her hair done in a series of braids that wound around her oval skull, sat at an organ to the left of the pulpit, playing soft funereal music.

Conversation suddenly stopped, and heads began turning toward the entrance. I looked to my right to see what had caused the sudden quiet.

Two men stood in the church door. The one in front was about five-eight, and looked like he weighed one-fifty stripped down. His black hair was slicked down like the doo wop singers of the sixties, and his pencil thin mustache looked waxed. He had skin the color of a mahogany piano, accented when he opened his mouth with pearly white teeth with dark spaces between them. A tan cashmere overcoat with white fur collar draped casually over his thin shoulders. The dark blue suit he wore over a baby blue silk shirt accented with a blood red tie looked like it cost more than I made in six months. In fact, the patent leather Italian shoes, in a dark red that was almost black, probably cost as much as all four tires on my Volkswagen. The guy in back looked like your ordinary, run-of-the-mill street thug. His bullet head was covered by reddish brown nappy hair, and he stared out at the world with narrow, ratty eyes under beetle brows. His broad nose had a bump halfway down the bridge from where it had been broken and not properly set. He was about six-one, and had to be carrying at least two hundred sixty pounds of solid muscle. His gray off-the-rack suit was stretched to the limits over his body, and I could see the bump of a pistol under his left arm.

A pimp and a street thug, my agile mind concluded. Other than the fact that they were about as welcome as pimples on prom night, I didn't see anything to justify the stunned silence.

"Who are the pimp and the muscle?" I whispered to Buster.

"Don't recognize either of them," he said, meaning he'd never arrested them, hauled them in for questioning, used them to get information, or been called to their aid.

That meant to me that they were non-entities, so the awed reception their presence caused was even more inexplicable. Their presence was tacky, but I couldn't see the reason for the reaction.

A broad-shouldered, broad-browed man with close cropped hair and soulful brown eyes set wide apart in his dark brown face rose from the left front pew and walked back to face the two new arrivals. He stood six feet tall, but the way he carried himself, he was able to face the goon without appearing to look up. He was dressed in a plain black suit that was shiny from wear, but he wore it with a quiet dignity.

The church wasn't all that large and the acoustics were first rate, so, even though he spoke in a quiet voice, I could hear him clearly.

"What are you doing here?" he asked in a

quiet, demanding voice.

Doo wop man looked up at him. There was a self-satisfied smirk on his face.

"Hey, man, I just come to pay my respects," he said. "This is my community, too, and I want Ochendele's family to know that I feel their loss."

"You are not welcome here, Mr. Coltrane, and this is *not* your community."

"Who is the guy confronting the newcomers?" I asked Buster in a hoarse whisper.

"That's Joseph Nkrumah," he whispered back. "He's sort of a community leader here in the African immigrant community. A real standup guy."

The 'standup' guy was standing up to the interlopers without flinching. Gave him points in my book. Of course, 'Coltrane' and his buddy weren't backing down either.

"Look, Joseph, my man," Coltrane said, making a whistling sound through the gaps in his teeth. "I'm just here to pay my respects to the family, you dig? I know with they man gone they gone be in need of help, and that's all I come to do. So, you let me deliver my condolences, and I blow this joint."

Nkrumah stood as stolid and solid as a

block of granite.

"You want me to move this turkey, Deacon?" the mass of muscle asked. He balled his ham-sized fists and started to move forward.

Coltrane laid a finely manicured hand on his muscular forearm.

"Naw, Kid, ain't no need for that," he said. "I'm sure Joseph here gone see reason. After all, I just come to help. How you think your people gone react, they find out I come with help and you turn me down? Or, do I have to have Billy move you aside?"

I could see that Nkrumah was wavering. That he intensely disliked Coltrane was obvious, but the offer he was making *sounded* sincere even to me. Heads were craned as several score pairs of eyes took in the tense tableau. Finally, Nkrumah sighed. "Very well," he said. "But, please do not waste time. The service will begin at any moment."

Coltrane took his time strolling toward the front of the church, his henchman in tow, looking from side to side as if he was some ancient potentate acknowledging the fealty of his subjects. He was met with vacant stares for the most part, a few snarls, though, were evident, especially from the men in the audience. Coltrane was becoming a puzzle, and I can't resist a puzzle. I didn't know if he had anything to do with Buster's problem, but he was becoming a figure of interest to yours truly.

He first went to the coffin, and stood looking down at the deceased for a few moments. Then, he turned. I would have sworn that he had a smug, satisfied look on his face, but it was only for a moment. Looking appropriately solemn, he approached a young woman in the right front pew – an attractive woman with caramel skin, her hair in neatly coiled braids, and immensely pregnant, with three children who barely came to her hips standing next to her, their wide eyes shiny with tears. They looked to be about a year apart in age, and the woman looked barely old enough to be their mother, with the black widow's dress she wore stretched across her tiny breasts. The only part of her that looked like a mature woman was her ample buttocks, which stretched the shiny black fabric to its maximum. Coltrane bowed slightly to the woman and placed a hand on her shoulder. She flinched and frowned, looking at his hand as if it was a spider, and there was a murmur in the crowd. Sensing that he'd overstepped some cultural boundary, Coltrane withdrew his hand and murmured something. He then reached into his jacket and pulled out an envelope. It was one of those white, business-sized envelopes, and it was thick. He handed it to the widow. When she opened it and looked down at the contents, she gasped loudly enough to be heard all the way in back where we were. There were gasps and murmurs from the people near her. She looked up at Coltrane, a broad smile illuminating her dusky face.

The smile of smugness returned to his face, and he flicked at the end of his mustache. Slowly, with his goon still following, glaring from side to side, he made his way back down the aisle toward the exit. He walked with his head held high and his shoulders squared, looking neither right nor left, but well aware of the changed expressions on the faces in the church.

As he passed, I thumped Buster on the forearm.

"Let's go, amigo," I said. "I've got to talk to this guy."

Three

Buster and I drew a few angry glares as we rushed out of the church.

We emerged from the building just as Coltrane was about to enter a light purple Cadillac Eldorado that was double parked next to the hearse. The big gorilla was holding the door.

"Mr. Coltrane," I yelled. "A word with you if you please."

He paused, partly in, partly out of the car, and looked back at me, a curious expression on his face. The gorilla gave us a menacing glower. As his right hand started toward his jacket, Buster pulled his own jacket open, showing his service weapon at his hip, and pulled the badge from his pocket, holding it up.

"I wouldn't even think about it, bub," he

said. "Don't want to give the undertaker more work on Sunday, now do we?"

Coltrane put a restraining hand on the big man's arm. "Take it easy, Kid, I'm sure Mr. Lawman just want to talk – right, Mr. Lawman?"

Buster looked at me, his eyebrows raised in a question. "Yes, we just want to talk," I said.

Coltrane looked at me, fingering his mustache.

"Now, Mr. Lawman here, he'd look like the man even without the badge. But, you don't look like the law to me. Why I want to talk to you?"

Okay, he had a point. He didn't have to talk to me. He didn't *have* to talk to Buster technically speaking. No laws that I knew of had been broken, other than the laws against good taste – showing up at a funeral in a purple pimpmobile should be illegal – we had no probable cause to do anything but let him go his way. But, there was something about him that gnawed at me.

"How about to satisfy my curiosity," I said. "For instance – you were clearly unwelcome inside there, but you came anyway. Why would you do that?"

"I just wanted to help a needy family in the neighborhood is all."

I didn't need to try and read him to know he was lying – I noticed the parking zone sticker on his windshield was for a zone in Southeast. I remembered it from a case I'd worked when I had to talk to a doctor in the area. "Now, that's strange," I said. "Especially considering you live in Anacostia."

His mouth gaped open. I knew what he was thinking – it happens a lot when I pick up on the things that most people don't notice. They think I'm some kind of psychic, when in fact I just pay attention.

"Uh, well . . . yeah, but the whole city is my neighborhood, know what I'm sayin'. That poor family wouldn't be able to pay they rent without help, and I was happy to help, dig. That's what I'm all about – helping my people."

His statement was a mish mosh of lies and truth. I could figure out that the comment about the family being unable to pay rent without help was the 'truth' part. The rest was pure bullshit – especially the part about *his* people.

"My, my, aren't you the generous one. And, just what do you get for your benevolence?"

"Get? What you talkin' 'bout, man? I told you, I just tryin' to help people what need it. I gets the satisfaction of helpin'."

Buster nudged me. "Where you goin' with

this, Al?" he asked quietly. "We ain't got time to try and figure out what scam this dirt bag's up to. We got important things to do."

"Hey, Mr. Lawman, ain't nice to talk 'bout a citizen like that. I got a mind to report you to my councilman."

Buster walked over and stared down at the little pimp. "Shit, turkey, you probably don't even know who your city councilmember is – unless you got him in your pocket."

The way Coltrane's eyes twitched said Buster had hit a sore spot. But, Buster had also been right. I was letting my obsession with puzzles divert me from what we'd really come for.

"You know, Buster, you're right. We're wasting time with Mr. Coltrane here." I turned to Coltrane, who was looking completely bewildered. "Thanks for your time."

"Yeah, little man," Buster said. "You can be on your way."

Coltrane's gorilla made a growling sound, and Coltrane's mouth turned down. But, he laid a hand on the thug's arm and shook his head. "Let's go, Billy," he said. "Officer, and Mr. whoever the fuck you are, ya'll have a nice day."

"The name's Pennyback, Al Pennyback," I said.

"Well, I'd like to say it's been nice to meet you, Mr. Pennyback," he retorted. "But, it ain't, so I guess I won't." He chuckled at his own wit.

He slid into the back seat. Billy the thug went around and got behind the wheel. The caddy made a throaty sound as he started the engine, but began to purr as he drove away.

The muted sounds from inside the church indicated that the service was ending. "Come on, bro," Buster said. "I got somebody I want you to talk to."

Death and Taxis

Four

Not wanting to disrupt the service, we stayed outside until it was over. The weather wasn't too cold, but we were both clapping our hands and stamping our feet by the time the pall bearers, followed by the preacher and the dead man's family, came through the door.

We followed the funeral procession to a cemetery about eight miles away. It was on a grassy knoll behind a six-foot high red brick fence – a peaceful area of flame trees and oaks dressed in yellow and orange, standing guard over row upon row of white markers on the grass that was now as much brown as green.

The widow, still clutching the purse containing Coltrane's generous donation to her chest, stood over the coffin wiping tears from her face. The children, looking lost and bewildered, stood next to her. The oldest one had tears streaming down his brown cheeks, but didn't cry aloud.

After hugging the widow and patting each of her kids on the head, Joseph Nkrumah walked over to where Buster and I stood at the back of the crowd of mourners who were there for the graveside service.

Up close, Nkrumah was even more somber looking and impressive than he'd been in the church confronting Coltrane. His deep brown eyes held both sadness and wisdom. The lines around his eyes told me he also had the years to have acquired both.

"Joe," Buster said. "This is a friend of mine, Al Pennyback. I've asked him to help me find out who's killing the cab drivers."

Then, it hit me. Joseph Nkrumah was one of Buster's informants. I don't know why it hadn't occurred to me earlier. I guess I was distracted by Coltrane.

Nkrumah stuck out his hand, and I grasped it. His palms were rough and callused – a man accustomed to hard labor.

"It is a pleasure to meet you, Mr. Pennyback," he said in a deep, resonant voice with that clipped English accent West Africans have. "If you can find the terrible person who is doing this, it will be a great service to the community."

There was a pleading look in his eyes. "I can't make any promises," I said. "The police think these murders are randomly committed acts; just murders committed in the course of robberies. In cases like that, it's very difficult to find those who did it. If the police are unable to solve it, it's unlikely I'll have much luck."

He shot Buster a querying look.

"I told him what we think," Buster said.

"Well, Mr. Pennyback, if Detective Mayweather has explained it to you, then you understand the problem we face in our community."

"He tells me that you think a gang of some kind is trying to move in," I said. "Maybe if you explained it to me from your perspective I would understand it better. What, for instance, makes you think that's what's happening?"

A look of impatience crossed his face. "Well, if you insist," he said. "We have had two taxi drivers from our community killed. The funeral today is for Mohammed Ochendele. He came here from Nigeria six years ago, and his three children were all born here. The other was Igor Meumi who arrived here from Cameroon just a year ago. He was saving to bring his wife and children over. They were killed a day apart, and after each, I received a phone call saying that it was a warning – if we didn't cooperate and allow them to operate in the neighborhood, there would be more."

"What kind of cooperation did they demand?"

"They were not very specific," he said. "Only that they would explain when I convinced the community to cooperate. But, I know what they want. They want our shops to serve as fronts for selling stolen goods and drugs, and they want to operate their houses of prostitution here. I know the type – we have many of them in our home countries in West Africa. Many of us came here to get away from that, and I cannot allow it to corrupt our young people who finally have a chance to have better lives than we did growing up back home."

There was conviction in his words. He didn't impress me as a man who gave in easily. "Do you have any idea who these people are?"

He shook his head in frustration. "No, the voices on the phone were different each time, and I could not identify them. Perhaps they were African, but they sounded very American. I could not tell you, though, whether they were black or white."

"But, why would they target cab drivers? I can't see how that would be of any use to them."

"I too am puzzled by that," he said. "It seems that they are trying to intimidate us, but to what end I cannot say. Perhaps they know that I'm the community leader, and people listen to me – and, I was once a taxi driver before deciding to devote full time to helping the community. I cannot say, for sure, but it is having an effect. Many are arguing for giving in. They feel that the authorities are of no help to us, or that because we are mere immigrants from poor African countries, they do not care, so we might as well cooperate in order to survive." He drove his left fist into his right palm with a smacking sound. "But, I cannot allow this to happen. We have worked too hard to build what we have. We have enough problems fending off Mr. Coltrane, and now we have this. We need help."

"What's your problem with Coltrane?" Buster asked. "Other than the fact that he smells up the place."

"Ah - Mr. Delmar Coltrane, who insists on being called Deacon, has been an irritant for the past six months. He wants to buy into most of the businesses here – become a partner. I have no proof, but there is a rumor that he is a dealer in stolen merchandise, along with charging outrageous interest rates for loans, and he wants to expand out of Anacostia into our African immigrant community."

I gave Buster a sharp look. "So, Mr. Pimpmobile is into loan sharking and fencing? I wonder why he's never popped up on your radar."

"Me too," Buster said, scowling. "I might just have to take a closer look at Mr. Coltrane's activities. 'Course, I been workin' violent gang crimes, and maybe he's avoided that kind of stuff. Maybe the burglary and confidence scheme units will have something on him. You think he's worth a look?"

If for no other reason than keeping his bad taste in automobiles off the community's streets he was worth a look. "Looks to me like you have two problems, Mr. Nkrumah," I said. I looked at Buster. "Putting the arm on Mr. Coltrane should at least solve one of them. In the meantime, I'd like everything you can get me on the gangs in town. Who is showing signs of expansion? I can't imagine something like this hasn't started some kind of buzz."

"Then, you will help us?" Nkrumah's expression was hopeful.

"I'll give it my best shot," I said.

Five

I was a bit depressed after attending the funeral, even though I'd never met the deceased. Funerals have that effect on me. Something about the smell of death that even the flowers can't erase – or maybe just the sad faces of the living, but it all depresses me. When I was a kid back in East Texas, my parents went to every funeral for every black person who died in our town, whether we knew them or not. Sitting there in a hot church house, with the smell of sweat and talcum powder, and the keening of mourners, many of whom also had never had a kind word for the deceased in life, always left me moody for days.

To make matters worse, the temperature dropped, so that by the time Buster dropped me off at home, my breath was forming little white vapors in front of my face as I walked from the yard to the porch. It was also getting late, and I'd not had lunch, so my stomach was growling. I'm grouchy when I'm hungry, and I don't like being cold. When I'm both, my day is real shitty.

Sandra was waiting for me – sitting on the couch with a blanket over her knees and a little parabolic heater on the floor at her feet. The room temperature was just this side of comfortable, but she hates being cold even more than I do, and even when I have the furnace turned up to max, she insists on extra blankets on the bed at night, *and* my warm body snugged up against hers. Actually, I sort of like the snuggling part, even when the weather's warm.

"Thank goodness you're back," she said as I stood in the door clapping my hands to get the circulation going. "I need your body heat."

"I need some heat inside," I said. "Why don't you join me in the kitchen while I rustle up some chow? If I don't eat something soon, my stomach will start gnawing on my ribs."

Wrapping the blanket around her shoulders, she followed me into the kitchen, and while I heated up a pot of leftover chili, she hung close to me. Rather than sitting opposite each other at the table, we went back into the living room and put the blanket over our laps and ate chili from the pot, washing it down with cold beer. The beer and chili eased the rumblings enough and warmed us both up. My day was starting to improve.

We gave it an hour to mostly digest and then did a quick wash and hit the blankets. Neither of us felt like doing anything but snuggling – but, that was enough.

We were awake at dawn the next morning, reluctant to crawl from beneath the blankets into the chilly air of the bedroom. But, both of us had been skipping on our exercise since the Thanksgiving binge at Buster and Alma's, so, groaning, we forced ourselves out of bed and skipped across the cold floor to the bathroom.

Dressed in grungy gray sweats and scuffed running shoes, we headed out for the woods in back of the house. I let Sandra run in front to start, mainly because I like the view. She's the only person I know who can look sexy in a dingy looking sweat suit, so whenever we run I always start out running behind her. She knows that's why I do it, too, so she puts a little extra sway on as she runs.

The leaves, coated with a layer of frost, made crunching sounds under our feet as we ran and our breathing preceded us in little white puffs that grew larger the longer we ran. The ground hadn't yet frozen, so it was still soft underfoot.

Overhead, the light blue of the sky was quite visible through the spider web network of bare branches.

We started out slow, picking up the pace a bit as we got deeper into the woods. The cold morning air stung the flesh of my face until I'd built up some body heat from the running. About a half mile into our run I pulled up even with Sandra. We were both running evenly now, our breath coming more easily. The condensation wrapped the lower parts of our faces.

Sandra is an athletic person, she'd always taken care of herself, but after taking up with me she'd really gotten into the whole PT thing – complete with morning runs, working out on the heavy bag, mastering martial arts, and meditation. She'd especially gotten into it after she effectively moved in with me at my farm house in suburban Maryland from her little frame house in the District's Takoma Park. She went back to her house about once or twice a week to check the furnace and water pipes and pick up mail, and now and then to replace the bulb in the lamp she kept burning in the living room. During the warm months, I swung by every weekend to cut her tiny lawn. Like me, she didn't subscribe to newspapers, so there was never the problem of newspapers piling up, although the occasional shopping inserts they toss out of cars had to be policed up. I don't think anyone was really fooled by any of that into thinking the house was occupied. Luckily, she had nothing much worth stealing, and hers was a neighborhood where people kept an eye on each other's houses, so it was never broken into.

We'd never discussed making our living arrangement permanent - it had just drifted in that direction. In fact, we rarely discussed our relationship, which was more or less exclusive by unspoken agreement. I love her; and, I was pretty sure she loved me. We'd actually used the 'L' word once or twice, but we didn't make a big deal of it, we just took each day as it came.

Sandra and I met when I was investigating the murder of a young man who had been one of her students at Carter, the inner city high school where she works. The police had put the teen's death down to street gang or drug activity, but his grandmother had disagreed and hired me to look into it. Sandra's neighbor, a retired executive who was moonlighting as an art thief, had tried to case blame her way, which put the two of into conflict – and which almost got the two of us killed. Fortunately, I'd solved the case, and we'd gotten beyond the head-butting. She'd become something more than just a fixture in my life. She had been the first woman that I'd had any kind of relationship with since the death of my wife a decade earlier, and had brought me out of my self-imposed exile from humanity, and showed me I could still have feelings. Since meeting her,

I hadn't been having the dreams about my dead wife and son as much, and when I did have them, they were no longer nightmares that left me sweating and crying.

We ran two miles out and two back, then did thirty minutes on the heavy bag in the barn behind the house. Sandra wanted to do some sparring to work on her martial arts form, giving me a workout that left us both sweating. Actually, I think she just felt like kicking my ass, which she did quite aggressively. The pupil was becoming as good as the teacher. After she pummeled me satisfactorily, we did twenty minutes of meditation, took hot showers, and fixed a big breakfast prior to going off to our respective jobs – her to Carter, and me to my office off Fourth Street in Southwest DC a few blocks north of the army's Fort McNair.

Sandra left first – she had hall monitor duties at her school, so she had to get there before the inmates, otherwise known as students, arrived. After cleaning up the kitchen, I fired up the green Volkswagen beetle she'd gotten me for my birthday, and struck out for my office. It was just a bit after seven, and traffic on River Road heading into DC was beginning to pick up. I took the Cabin John Parkway exit where River Road crosses the Beltway – traffic was picking up there too, but nothing compared to the snarl of vehicles on I-495. Cabin John merges into Clara Barton Parkway and then into Canal Road, a two-lane road that winds along the old C&O Canal, with a steep hill on the left and occasional views of the Potomac River on the right, which emerges into the District and becomes M Street on the southern edge of the Georgetown University campus. Just before Francis Scott Key Bridge I took the exit onto Whitehurst Freeway. I got off Whitehurst near Twenty-Seventh Street and did the loop around to Rock Creek and Potomac Parkway which goes past the classic white structure of the Kennedy Center for the Performing Arts, which sits overlooking the Potomac. I enjoy the bucolic scenery on Canal Road and the parkways, but the sight of the monuments out of the left window as I drove past the Lincoln Memorial, got to me as always. Gleaming white marble reflecting the sun's rays, the memorials to Lincoln, Washington, and Jefferson symbolize what the country is supposed to be all about better than anything I can think of. The fact that out of the right window I can also see the green, peaceful looking hillside of Arlington National Cemetery, where so many of the people who paid the ultimate sacrifice for that country was also not lost on me. No matter how many times I made that drive, it always got to me.

Once past the Lincoln Memorial and across Independence Avenue, the scenery changes, from gleaming white marble and majestic buildings done in Greek architecture, to red, brown and yellow brick utilitarian structures with a decidedly more industrial look. When you get on Maine Avenue and cross under I-395, with the Fish Market on your right, you know you're in a working class neighborhood by the smell as much as the outward appearance. The Fish Market's odor is not as noticeable when the weather's cold as it is in summer, but it never completely goes away, and seeps into the car even with the windows rolled up. There have been efforts to gentrify the area, with a few high-rise condos going up here and there, but it's still dominated by one and two-story buildings that are stained from years of neglect and pollution, with sidewalks populated by people who look beaten down and forgotten. And, they look that way because they have been beaten down and forgotten.

My office is in an old two-story building that looks like one of those roadside motels you see when you drive south. The owners recently painted it, but sitting in the shadow of new pink stone high rise apartments, it looks like what it is – a relic of a bygone time clinging precariously to its place. It still has a small parking lot, though, and each tenant has two reserved places for staff and one for customers. I pulled the Bug into my accustomed spot next to my assistant Heather Bunche's blue Honda Civic. Our visitor's slot was, as usual, empty. What walk-in business we get is usually from people who take the bus. I walked quickly to the top of the stairs on the right that lead up to the little balcony that runs the width of the building. The pile of lumber, empty cans, and packing crates from the painting job were still stacked haphazardly in front of the empty end unit.

Also as usual, Heather was already there when I arrived. Sometimes I suspected she slept in the office just to be able to beat me in. I know she didn't, but I couldn't keep the thought from popping into my head from time to time.

Heather and I have been working together from the beginning – more than a decade now. After my old army buddy Quincy Chang convinced me to stop sitting around feeling sorry for myself and become a private detective, and then sweetened the deal by convincing his law firm to put me on a lucrative retainer for the occasional odd job, I realized that doing the paperwork required to run even a one-man operation wasn't my strong suit. Heather Bunche, a tiny, bubbly blonde had just graduated from secretarial school and was in need of work. I hired her midway through the interview, and when I discovered that she was also a magician when it came to coaxing data from computers and information from her network of fellow secretaries and personal assistants, I realized that our association was a match made in heaven.

She'd shared a few dangers with me over the years, and had been instrumental in solving more than one case, so I'd been grooming her for the past two years to apply for her PI license so I could make her a full partner in A.E. Pennyback, Confidential Enquiries. I'd considered changing the name to reflect her new status, but she talked me out of it. It had, she said, to do with our 'brand.' I didn't have a clue what she was talking about, but figured if she was okay with leaving things alone I would be as well.

She was sitting at her desk when I walked in. A cup of some kind of flowery smelling tea was at her elbow, and a stack of booklets spread out in front of her. Her computer screen was lit up, but she wasn't peering at it or pecking at the keyboard as she usually does.

"Hey, kiddo," I said as I started shucking my jacket. "What's with all the paper? I thought you did everything electronically."

She turned to look at me. A lock of her blonde hair flopped over one blue eye, giving her the appearance of peeking at me with the other eye.

"I'm studying for getting my license," she said. "And, there's not much of use on the Internet, so I have to use paper books." She said it as if somehow reading an *actual* book as opposed to looking at it on a computer screen was somehow sinful.

"You don't have to take an exam, kid. You

mainly just fill out a few forms. You've already finished the training."

She'd done more than 60 hours of training – I'd had to join her for eight hours of in-service refresher to renew my own tickets – covering the laws of DC, Virginia and Maryland, investigative techniques, and gotten her weapon certification as well. Neither of us carried a weapon – didn't even own one – but got the certification just to be covered. Because of the number of self-important politicians and other bigwigs in the DC metro area, regulations on private security firms and people are among the strictest in the nation. Anyone wanting to do security work almost has to get licensed by all three to stay out of trouble. It costs about four hundred bucks a year for each license, or just over two grand for both of us when the refresher training is included, but the retainer from Quincy's firm would easily cover it.

In addition to the training and weapons certificates, Heather had to submit fingerprint cards and was subject to a criminal records check. That was no problem – she didn't even have a traffic violation on her record. The applications for Maryland and Virginia would be mailed to Pikesville and Richmond respectively, but we'd decided to go to the DC Metro Police station on Fourteenth Street where the private security management branch issued PI and security guard licenses and get the DC ticket in person. Just as a matter of courtesy, and because I like bantering with the tough sergeant in charge, I always go there in person to get my renewal done every year.

Heather pushed the books away. "I know," she said. "But, I can't help but worry that when I turn my paperwork in they'll think of something to ask me, and I won't know the answer."

In addition to being a computer whiz, Heather is something of a worry wart. She's usually worried about me and the shenanigans I get up to on the street, though. It was strange seeing her worried about herself for a change.

"Don't sweat it. They don't work that way. You got the paperwork in order and can pay the fee, so it's a snap. We're not going until Wednesday, so why don't you stop worrying about it. I've got us a case – from Buster of all people – so, why don't you use that brain of yours on it instead of fretting over your license?"

She shot me a look that was nine parts skepticism – I'm seldom the one to get us a new case. "And, just what kind of case did *you* stumble across, boss man?"

I gave her a quick rundown. I suggested she start first with looking into the backgrounds of the two victims, and at the same time get as much as she could on the murders of all the cab drivers. As an afterthought, I gave her

Coltrane's name and asked her to see what she could dig up on him. It might come in useful when I got around to dissuading him from poking his nose into the African community. As I spoke I could see her interest perking up, and by the time I gave her a summary of the enigmatic Coltrane and his purple pimpmobile, she was fairly salivating with a desire to start mining the world wide web for the bits and bytes of data that represented the lives, hopes, loves, and failures of everyone even remotely associated with the case.

Few people realize the amount of information about their personal lives exists in the computerized files of companies and organizations around the world – your credit card purchases, reading preferences, arrest records – you name it, and chances are someone has created a digital file and stored it somewhere for people like Heather to retrieve all the bytes and pieces and stitch them back together to create a comprehensive profile that can be used to track you down, or even predict what you might do under certain circumstances. Using data mining techniques, that no matter how she tried to explain them I never understood, someone can find out things about you that you might not even know yourself. If you're the paranoid type it could keep you up nights.

That, anyway, is what Heather tells me. I left her to it. She never seems happier than when she's pecking away at her keyboard, making her computer screen dance with an ever-changing display of data, and when she's happy, I'm happy.

I knew she'd forgotten the PI license application, when she began humming an unidentifiable melody and absent-mindedly sipping at her tea. I went into my office.

Slightly smaller than the outer office, mine at least had the advantage of a window with a view. The window was behind me, forcing me to swivel my chair around to see, and the view for most of the year was the sleek sides of the high-rise condos that stood between us and the Washington Channel. Only in late fall and winter, when the trees that had been planted in the plazas between the condos were stripped of their leaves, could I actually see the channel, and a little sliver of the Potomac River beyond that. It hadn't gotten too cold for the diehard sailors, and I could see the limp sails of dozens of boats tied up in the channel. There was even one early morning sailor gliding southward with sails fully expanded in the cold morning air. The sun's rays, reflected from the polished walls of the high rises, were a warm gold.

I swung my chair back from the window, taking in my office as I rotated. Not much to see really. Muted pastel coloring on the wall – sometimes it looks brown, at others, depending on the angle of the light, almost a subtle purple

– an autographed photograph of me with General Colin Powell when he was Chairman of the Joint Chiefs of Staff and I was a lieutenant colonel assigned to the Pentagon. The photo had been taken just weeks before my wife and son were killed in an auto accident, and I retired from the army – and for a long time, from life. It was one of the few physical reminders of that period of my life I hung onto. Heather had found a couple of hunting prints and had them framed, and that constituted my wall decorations. There was a plain wooden chair in front of my desk. I didn't encourage visitors to stay long. My own chair was a nice leather executive chair I'd picked up at an auction. A bit scuffed, but it had character. My desk was standard government-issue executive desk – dark brown wood with two drawers on either side in which I kept very little. I'd picked the desk up at an auction of excess government property for about twenty bucks. A bookcase to my left, containing a few volumes of military history, a signed copy of Powell's *My American Journey*, and copies of the relevant laws of DC, Maryland, and Virginia that a PI needs to be aware of, completed the furnishings.

A computer sat in the center of my desk. I hardly ever used it, and then only to check my mail and play computer chess. I left the serious stuff to Heather.

The computer made little whirring and chirping noises as it warmed up. When it quit flickering I opened my email folder. Nothing of interest, so, after deleting everything, I closed it and started a chess game. I have to admit I'm something of a masochist in this regard. I'd never beaten the computer, but I kept coming back again and again like the Vegas gambler who keeps putting chips on 'Even' at roulette because the book on 'How to Win at Roulette' told him that was the way to beat the house. It never works in Vegas, and it had yet to work for me. I could sometimes imagine the damn machine sitting there quietly laughing down inside its circuits at my vain efforts.

I was well into a game – my King was in jeopardy – when the intercom light on my phone lit up. I 'paused' the game and pressed the answer button.

"Yeah, Honeybunch – what's up?" I used the pet name she would only let *me* use – and then only sparingly.

"I got the first flow of information on the names you gave me. You want a data dump?"

"Yeah," I said. "You want me to come out there?"

She answered by breaking the connection.

I shut the game down and watched as the screen started to go dim, signaling that the computer was going to sleep. I got up and went out to her desk. She'd pulled her visitor's chair

– a more comfortable seat than the one in my office – around so I could see her computer screen.

The document showing was a news report with a grainy black and white photo that I didn't recognize at first – then, I saw it was a photo of Coltrane. I pointed at the screen.

"You recognize him?" she asked.

"That's the guy who showed up at the funeral . . . Coltrane."

"Yes, Delmar Coltrane," she said. "Prefers to be called Deacon for reasons I simply cannot fathom."

"I pegged him as a small time grifter who's tryin' to get his hooks into the businesses in the immigrant community."

She waggled a finger at me. "Really? That's not the way he's portrayed in the media. The community papers, and sometimes even the *Washington Post*, paint him as some kind of angelic benefactor. He supports homeless shelters, neighborhood sports teams – all kinds of charities. I can't find anything else on him – no police record – no nothing."

"So, the guy's rich," I said. "Maybe he's trying to invest as a way to use his money."

"That, boss is why I have him on the screen first. If the news reports are correct, there's no doubt that he's *rich*. There's just one little problem. None of the reports say where his money comes from. He isn't CEO or owner of any registered business."

"Maybe he inherited it."

"I already thought of that," she said. No surprise there – Heather rarely leaves a stone unturned in her quest for information. "I dug as deep as I could in such a short time, and I came up with one little tidbit that makes that unlikely. He is an orphan. He was raised in a series of foster homes until he turned eighteen. If he had rich relatives, why would they let that happen?"

Why indeed. "Okay, he doesn't own a business, and he didn't have a rich uncle. Where does his money come from? I was told that there's suspicion he's into fencing stolen goods."

"He must be moving a lot. Last year he gave a million dollars to Big Brothers alone. You'd think, though, if he was involved in criminal activity he'd have a record, but I did a cursory check and as far as I can tell, he's never even gotten a parking ticket. The guy's clean as a whistle."

Now, she had my attention. Mr. Delmar 'Deacon' Coltrane just moved to the head of my 'persons of interest list.' He was more than a simple puzzle – he had become a full-blown enigma wrapped in a conundrum, and I was determined to solve it. On the one hand, he seemed to get off on being 'Mr. Generous,' but at the same time he was strong arming the merchants of the community for a share in their business. The Jekyll-Hyde persona was confusing.

Getting to the bottom of the Coltrane mystery would do nothing to solve the murders of the cab drivers, or identify the gang or gangs trying to muscle into the neighborhood, but with Heather on the case, reconstructing Coltrane's history wouldn't detract from it either – or so I convinced myself.

"Okay, here's what I want you to do," I said. "Do a deep dive into Mr. Coltrane. I want to know everything there is to know about him from the day he was born. He's up to something, and my gut tells me it's not for the good of the community. Did you get anything on the two dead cab drivers?"

Other than confirming what Joseph Nkrumah had told me, nothing much. Both men were legal immigrants, upstanding citizens with clean records. The only thing that flagged their deaths in my mind was that both had been killed in parts of the city not usually associated with criminal activity – Ochendele near the intersection of Utah Avenue and Barnaby Street after dropping off a fare he'd picked up at National Airport, and Meumi near

Foxhall Road and Greenwich Parkway west of Georgetown University. Both were upscale residential neighborhoods where the main crime tended to be kids spray painting graffiti on the sides of buildings, and an occasional car break-in. The other killings had been in Southeast and Northeast – unfortunately, parts of the District where violent crimes are all too common.

The killings had all been similar. The victims' throats had been cut, leaving them to bleed out. The publicly available reports indicated that police believed they'd been attacked by someone sitting in the backseat of their cabs. There were indications that the weapons in each case were different, which led police to believe this was the work of random perpetrators. While it was certainly possible, I wasn't convinced. It didn't make sense that a robber would be waiting in an area of expensive homes in Northwest DC to be picked up by a taxi, or in the ritzy area of Georgetown where the second driver was killed. No witnesses came forward in any of the incidents – not surprising in the working class areas of Southeast and Northeast, but unusual in the Northwest.

So, with little else to go on, I was nonetheless convinced that Buster and Nkrumah were right – there was definitely something fishy about the whole thing. I told Heather to do a search of all crimes against taxi drivers for the past year to see if she could detect a pattern. At the same time, I asked her to be on the lookout for any signs of gangs combining or any other suspicious gang activity.

That didn't really leave much for me to do. Unlike the cops, or the private eyes you see in the movies, I don't have a battalion of snitches and informants lurking about in alleys and pool halls waiting to pass along the information I need to solve a case. I just have me and Heather – mostly Heather. She's my inside 'man,' and I'm my muscle. She skips her fingers over her keyboard, coaxing the electrons to give up their information, or flips through her address book for just the right phone number of just the right person in the office that happens to have the bit of data we need, and then she coaxes it from them like a magician pulling a pigeon from a hat. I, on the other hand, must rely on shoe leather and muscle. I walk the streets, knock on doors, and on occasion knock a few heads together to get the information I need.

It's not elegant, but it works for us. Well, it works for me. Heather's not too much for the head-knocking part.

Death and Taxis

Six

Heather and I spent the rest of the day comparing notes – meaning I popped out to her desk every few hours to discover that she'd dug up nothing new on the case, leaving me to sit behind my desk and stew, and leaving her, after the third time, to suggest that I go home and leave her to work in peace.

I quit in disgust just before five and lit out for home, leaving her to close up shop.

The heavy end-of-day traffic heading out of Washington did nothing to lighten up my mood. By the time I finally pulled to a stop outside the house, I was in a blue funk.

Entering the living room, I was brought up short. Sandra, who had gotten out of school early for a change and beat me home, was also in a blue funk. Figuring there was no sense in both of us stewing, I took a deep breath and asked her what was wrong – and regretted it as soon as the words were out of my mouth.

You see, Sandra is very interested in politics. I mean, very, very interested. She frets over even local elections. Discusses it endlessly with her students in an effort to make them more aware of their responsibilities as citizens. She doesn't often bring it home because she knows that other than voting I think very little of politics, and even less of politicians.

The elections that were conducted earlier in the month, though, had really captured her imagination. She'd been a strong Clinton supporter, despite some of his personal failings, and like many District residents was a staunch Democrat. The election between Clinton's VP, Al Gore, and Bush, the governor of Texas and son of a former president, had been important to her. I'd voted for Gore, using the principle better the devil you know than the one you don't, and had promptly purged my mind of the whole thing.

I hadn't been following the news, though, and it turned out that the elections weren't over on November 7 when the polls closed.

In Florida the two candidates were in a see-saw battle, and the vote was so close nationwide, the outcome in Florida could decide the election. And, that was what had her in a snit. Seems it had whipped back and forth from one to the other several times, until it was decided to let the courts decide. Seems the democratic candidate had demanded a recount because of questionable ballots, and the republican had gone to court to block the recount. State officials, loyal to the republican side, had declared the results of their state favored their candidate, sending the democrats to court to contest their decision.

In other words, it was a royal mess, and looking likely that the republicans would win, and Sandra was fuming about 'wasted votes,' and the like.

Sort of made my frustration over lack of leads in the taxi driver murder case look petty, so I rubbed her back and made soothing noises, took her out to dinner at one of our favorite Thai restaurants in Fairfax, and then gave her a full body massage when we got home.

She was feeling marginally better by the time we drifted off to sleep, which gave my mind the opportunity to drift back onto my problem. And, that's when the dream began.

I found myself in a place that . . . wasn't exactly a place. At least, not in a physical sense, because except for the semi-solid feel of ground – or whatever it was – under my feet, there were no landmarks, walls, or anything to give it form or substance. There was no sound other than the whisper of my breathing. I was surrounded by a swirling gray fog – a billowing blanket of insubstantial vapor – that obscured even my feet. But for the feel of whatever it was that I stood upon, I could have been floating in an amorphous sea of nothingness.

The dream always began this way. I hadn't had it often lately – for several years in fact – but, it came back whenever I was deeply troubled.

And, as usual, I found myself moving forward. Not walking in the traditional sense. More like gliding forward on a moving conveyor belt. As I moved forward, the fog cleared, and I was in a wooded glade. Surrounded by deep, lush greenery; a green carpet of moss beneath my feet. Somewhere in the distance toward which I was still moving, I could hear the musical tinkle of flowing water.

Eventually I came to the banks of a stream. Neither wide nor narrow, it seemed, though, impassable – or so my mind informed me. I stood there waiting as I always did until a figure began to appear.

Slowly the figure resolved itself into my late wife, Sarah. Short, but well formed, her round, brown face gleaming in a light that seemed to come from everywhere and nowhere, she regarded me with her dark brown eyes, and I felt a lump in my chest – a burning longing for what could never be again. The sting of tears caused me to blink. I reached out for her. She smiled that angelic smile of hers.

"Al, my darling." Her lips didn't move, but her voice was crystal clear in my mind. *"You are troubled again."*

I don't know – never knew – if my lips moved, but I told her about the case. As the words tumbled out, she nodded, still smiling. When I was finally finished, she nodded.

"Things are never what they first seem, Al," she said. *"You taught me that; remember. The answer is always close at hand, but you're looking too far away."*

Her answer made less sense than they usually did, but somehow it comforted me. Sarah had that ability when she was alive, and as a – I couldn't bring myself to call her a ghost – whatever she was; she still made me feel better about things. I'd come to terms with being unable to touch her, so I no longer woke up sweating and fighting the blankets.

As her image faded, along with the green glade and stream, to be replaced by the gray fog just before I woke, I smiled.

I was smiling when I woke up to feel the warmth of Sandra's body spooned up against mine. I still didn't have any answers, and didn't have a clue where to start looking for answers, but it no longer bothered me.

I lay there looking up at the ceiling for an hour before poking Sandra in the ribs to wake her up for our morning exercise.

We were in the middle of breakfast when my cell phone chimed. It was Buster.

"Hey, bro," his booming voice echoed in my ear as his words tumbled out. "We got another murder. Another cab driver – another of my CIs. It's over near the Fish Market off Maine Avenue. You want to meet me there?"

"Okay, Buster," I said. "I'm just finishing breakfast. Give me an hour."

That would be pushing it, but it wasn't yet seven-thirty, and if I beat the traffic crossing the two main bridges from Northern Virginia, I could just make it.

I actually made it in fifty-five minutes.

Buster was already waiting for me just outside the yellow crime scene tape. He was talking to a bored looking uniformed officer who nonetheless kept a wary eye on the cars on Maine Avenue that slowed down to get a look.

I parked behind a DC police cruiser with its red and white flashing lights, and walked over to Buster.

"Hey, Al," he said as he lifted the tape and stepped under it, holding it for me. "Glad you could make it."

The uniformed officer, a young black dude with a pencil thin mustache and light green eyes, nodded at me as I passed.

"So, what you got?" I asked.

We were approaching a red and blue cab that was partially on the curb. Even from ten feet away I picked up the metallic odor of blood. As I got closer, I could see that the driver's side was awash in blood, which was congealing and turning dark. A stoop-shouldered guy with dirty blond hair in need of cutting and a paunch that begged for a few sessions in a gym stood near the cab talking to another uniform. His suit looked off the rack – in the bargain basement section of the store – dark blue and shiny at the elbows. When he saw Buster and me approaching, his sour look became downright bitter.

"What are you doing here, lieutenant?" he asked in a reedy voice that was full of contempt. "This case doesn't concern your unit."

"And, good morning to you too, captain," Buster said. He turned to me – a mischievous smile on his face. "Al, this is Captain Robert Helsing, chief of the street crime task force. Captain, this is Al Pennyback, ace detective and a friend of mine."

Helsing gave me a look you'd normally reserve for the dog crap you accidentally stepped in. "Lieutenant Mayweather, you know better than to involve a civilian in an active crime scene – and in particular one that is not your responsibility to investigate."

Buster leaned in toward the man, who stood five inches shorter and was probably forty pounds lighter. "It does concern me," he said. "I know this cab number. The driver's a guy named Dudu Nkomo. I assume the morgue guys have already removed the body, but my guess is his throat was cut like all the others. He was, by the way, another of my CIs."

"Ah, well," Helsing said, blinking. "Be that as it may, this is still *my* case, and your presence is not only unauthorized, it's not welcome." He turned to me. "And, as for you, Mr. Pennyback, you have no right to be here regardless of the circumstances, so if you don't want me arresting you for interfering with my investigation, you'll get over there beyond the tape."

I briefly considered arguing with the idiot, but it might end up getting Buster in trouble, and I didn't want that. With my license renewal coming up, when I thought about it, it wasn't a good idea to toy with being arrested either. I gave Buster a nod and a wink and walked back to the yellow tape and slipped underneath. It didn't matter. I could still hear them clearly, and I could see all I needed to see from where I stood. The smell of blood was so strong up close, and brought back so many unpleasant memories, I was actually more comfortable outside the tape, and Helsing had a look of smug satisfaction on his vulpine face, so maybe he'd ease up on Buster a bit. Yeah, and water's not wet. The asshole was still trying to bully Buster into leaving. Now, that was a pretty dumb thing to do. Buster Mayweather is not a guy you want to bump chests with.

"You didn't answer my question, captain," Buster said. His voice was tight. If Helsing hadn't been so dumb, he would have noticed. "Was the MO in this case the same as the others?"

"I don't have to answer your questions, *lieutenant*." Buster moved in closer. Now, Helsing was beginning to get the message. His face paled. "But, as a matter of fact, yes, this driver's throat was cut, and it looks like whoever did it was in the back seat."

Death and Taxis

Seven

For a few moments I thought Buster might bust Helsing in the chops anyway, but he just shrugged and walked over to where I stood.

"Hey, bro," he said. "I'm starvin', why don't we head over to Mom's for a soul food breakfast?"

I'd already eaten, but because of his call had missed my second cup of coffee. I flipped out my phone and called Heather to let her know I'd be late – and explained that I was working a lead on the case.

I followed him back up Maine Avenue to Fourteenth Street, then north to Chinatown where we cut over to Sixteenth Street and up to U Street. The breakfast crowd was heavy with black and Hispanic laborers grabbing a bite before going off to whatever jobs they'd picked up for the day. Buster parked in front and put a 'Police Business' sticker on his dash. He directed me to the empty spot behind him and handed me an extra sticker for the Bug's dash.

We went inside. Our usual table in the corner with a view of both the interior of the place and the sidewalk outside was free, and mom – all three hundred pounds of her – was sitting at her usual place near the cash register.

"Well, Lawdy mercy," she said in her little girl voice. "First time I done seen you two in so early. Come to try Mom's special breakfast, have you?"

"You got that right," Buster said. "You just bring me double of everything."

She beamed – she liked nothing better than hearing something like that – and looked at me. "I've already eaten," I said. "But, I will have a cup of coffee."

Her beam was replaced by a frown. "You can't come in here and just drink coffee," she said. "How 'bout you have a biscuit and gravy with that coffee?"

I shrugged. I could run it off. Besides, Mom's biscuits and brown gravy literally melt in your mouth, and even though I know the American Medical Association would disapprove, she uses real lard in the gravy and chicken fat stock to make the gravy. "Okay, but just one," I said. Her smile came back.

She waddled off toward the kitchen. Buster and I took our seats, me with my back to the wall as usual, him to my right where he still had a good view of our surroundings.

"Well, what did you think of the crime scene?" he asked. "Don't this whole think strike you as a little bit hinky?"

"I think these killings are . . . as you say . . . hinky. The first two weren't killed by some robbery gang lying in wait. No way could that happen in those two neighborhoods without someone noticing. If this guy Helsing comes up with no witnesses in today's killing, I'd put that in the hinky category as well. There's always someone in the fish market, so someone has to have seen something."

"Now, that's what I'm talkin' 'bout," he said. "I knew you'd see something that fool missed."

As I basked in the glow of his compliment, Mom came out with a big plastic tray laden with a breakfast big enough to feed a rifle squad. She put most of it in front of Buster. Sausage, bacon, biscuits and gravy, scrambled eggs, fried tomatoes, hash browns – the whole shebang – along with a huge mug of coffee. A plate with a single biscuit covered in light brown gravy, and a cup of her steaming hot coffee was put in front of me.

"If you eat all that, they'll have to send a tow truck to pull you out of here."

"Shit, dude – I'll burn most of this off the first gang banger I have to chase down. This is the kind of breakfast a man is supposed to eat. Now, tell me what you plan to do 'bout this case."

"Well, I actually plan to do two things," I said. "First, I'll do what I can to try and find out who's killing the cabbies. But, I also plan to dissuade Mr. Coltrane from sticking his nose into the community's affairs."

"Why you want to worry 'bout some penny ante fool like Deacon Coltrane?" he asked around a mouthful of bacon. "Joseph 'been takin' care of him."

"Well, it's not like I'm being paid for the first job. Just call Coltrane a pro bono on top of my pro bono for you. Besides, I don't like the man."

He continued to fork food into his mouth, regarding me intently. Finally, he put his fork down, washed down his food with a giant gulp of coffee and leaned across the table toward me.

"I been knowin' you too long, Al," he said. "You got something else on your mind, now spill."

I think the thought had been hovering on

the fringes of my consciousness all along – had been tickled by the dream – and now, with him pressing me, it took on form. "I have a feeling about Mr. Coltrane, Buster. Nothing specific, but don't you think it's a bit more than coincidence that soon after he tries to move in on the business in the area, these killings start?"

He leaned back, looking at me skeptically.

"Come on. You tellin' me you think Coltrane's behind the killings? That he's involved in some gang? The man ain't got a rap sheet. If he was into gang stuff, we'd of tumbled to it before now."

"When you put it like that, I admit it sounds a bit illogical," I said. "But, I don't believe in coincidence. There has to be some connection – I'll just have to find it.

No way was I about to tell him I'd come to this conclusion because of a dream. He's a friend, but even friendship has its limits. He thought me eccentric. I didn't want him thinking I was crazy.

"Now, tell me about today's victim. You said his name was . . . what?"

"Dudu, and yeah, it's pronounced doo doo," he said. He spelled it. "I know it sounds freaky, but the guy came from Zimbabwe, and over there they have some real freaky names. His last name is . . . was Nkomo. He pronounced it 'In-komo. Why you want to know 'bout him?"

"I'm having Heather run everyone down – trying to see if there are any connections, anything in their backgrounds that caused them to be selected as victims."

"You don't think they might just be randomly selected to scare the shit out of people?"

That was always a possibility. It was a page right out of the old Maoist revolutionary playbook, and had been refined by modern day terrorist groups. Random killings had a way of putting the fear of God into a population simply *because* of their randomness. The problem for me was it didn't seem to strike me as the way gangs operated. There was something I was missing.

"That's always possible," I conceded. "But, until I check every possibility, I'm not prepared to accept that as the main hypothesis."

"Half the time, bro, I don't know what the hell you sayin'," he said. He shook his head and laughed. "But, you get results, and that's what counts. What you want me to do?"

I needed whatever information the police had on the cab drivers and other people in the immigrant community, including Joseph Nkrumah, his take on gang activity in the area –

and, anything else he could dig up from police files that might have bearing on the case.

"While you're at it, you could look into Coltrane. Heather found a little on him – for one thing, the guy's rolling in dough, but we can't find out how he gets it. I'd like to know what kind of business he's in.

Then, just before I decided that watching him eat all that food was threatening to cause me to eat a second breakfast; something I didn't need to do, I had another thought.

"One more thing, pal," I said. "Could you check with the cab companies and find out where they made pickups around the time they were killed?"

"My three CIs?"

"No, all of them."

"Why you want to know about the others?"

"Call it a hunch," I said. "But, there just might be a connection that both you and Helsing are missing."

I left him looking confused. When I got back into my car, I took the 'Police Business' sign and threw it into the glove compartment, hoping he wouldn't remember giving it to me. You never know when something like that might come in handy.

Death and Taxis

Eight

It was nearly nine by the time I got to the office. Heather was pecking at her keyboard. She looked up and smiled brightly when I came in.

She had a cup of tea at her left elbow and a steno pad at her right. Now and then, she'd turn away from the computer and make notes in the pad in her precise script, nodding as she wrote.

"Glad you finally woke up and decided to come to work," she said without looking up.

"I've been up for a while. Had breakfast at Mom's with Buster."

That brought her head up. She looked at me quizzically. "What brought that on?"

I told her about the murder of another cab driver – another of Buster's CIs.

"Two's a coincidence, three's a conspiracy," she said.

I winced. Heather is beautiful. She's smarter than a room full of Mensa members. But, she sucks at telling jokes. But, the weakness of her attempt aside, she was right.

"Yeah, there's something foul afoot," I said. "And, we have to come up with a plan to expose it."

"Well, I checked the two cab drivers whose names you gave me – they had pretty clean records. Same thing for Joseph Nkrumah. He started out as a cabbie, but then quit his job and works full time on behalf of the community. He lives on whatever the community donates. Just hard working immigrants trying to live the American dream as far as I can tell."

Someone was trying to turn their American dream into a nightmare. That pissed me off. I hate people who exploit others. But, hate's not a good investigative approach, so I took a deep breath and cleared my mind.

"I want you to run a check on the latest victim," I said. "And, while you're at it, see if you can get cab company records showing pickups on the days of the murders."

"I thought you asked Buster to do that?"

"I did, but I asked him for the pickups around the time of the killings. I want you to get the whole day – for all of the murdered drivers, not just Buster's guys. I want to see if maybe there's some pattern to their movements that might have bearing on the case. I asked Buster to dig up whatever he can find out about Coltrane, but I'd like you to take another run at him as well. See if you can find out what kind of business he's in."

She gave me a pouty look. I was asking her to take on a huge task. A cabbie might pick up ten to twenty fares during a shift – even more if he does a lot of short hauls during rush hour. Combing through the fare logs of seven drivers would take a lot of time, and that was assuming the companies they worked for kept neat records, and would be willing to share them with us. She pouted, but she'd do it.

The next step was to lay out an investigative plan. The way I saw it, I was doing two investigations. Scaring Deacon Coltrane off was the easy one. I'd just find out where he hung out, get some details on his rackets, and then tell him bluntly to go graze in other pastures. The goon he had driving him around might try to get in the way, but I've handled bigger, tougher guys than him. The harder job was getting to the bottom of the cabbie murders.

I had to somehow establish motive, means, and opportunity. With these, I'd be a step ahead in identifying the culprit, or since Buster was sure this was gang related, the culprits. Once I did that, Buster and I could sit down and decide what to do about them. Most likely, he'd get a few of his buddies on the force and take the perps down – probably in a public manner that would not only remove the danger to the community, but would leave Captain Robert Helsing with egg all over his face. I could live with that.

Motive *seemed* clear. Kill the drivers in order to instill fear in the community, making it easier for the gang to move in. Nothing, however, is as it first appears to be. There were easier ways for a gang to move in on a neighborhood. This seemed so Machiavellian and convoluted – beyond the mental capacity and inclination of your average gang. There had to be some other motive – something that was probably staring us in the face, but that was so obvious we were missing it. I was hoping the pickup logs would shed some light on other possible motives.

The means was known – someone had used a sharp knife to open each man's jugular, leaving him to bleed out in seconds.

From what Heather had picked up, there was no sign of struggle, indicating that each victim had been caught unawares and killed before he could fight back, or that the victims knew their killer. Given the number and lack of relationship among the seven victims, the latter seemed unlikely. That left the possibility of the killer being an innocent looking fare the drivers had picked up. The one thing all of the victims *did* have in common was that they were gypsy drivers – freelance drivers as opposed to fulltime employees of a company. The vehicles they drove weren't equipped with the Plexiglas partitions between front and rear seats, making it relatively easy for someone in the back seat to reach over and grab them from behind – which pretty much covered opportunity as well.

It looked like we'd have to work from the easy ones – means and opportunity – in hopes of stumbling upon motive.

Whenever I had one of those cases that looked like a gigantic stonewall with no doors and that stretched so far in both directions there was no practical way around it, in addition to meditating to clear my mind, I had my go-to guy for the impenetrable enigmas. Carlton 'Blood' Raine was a septuagenarian retired CIA agent who lived in a log cabin in the woods out beyond where I lived. He was one of the first black field agents in what had been until that time pretty much a buttoned-down good old boy organization, and had earned his nickname 'Blood' because of his capacity for doing wet work – a euphemism for gunfire, knife-work, and other methods of dispatching your opponent. After retirement, Blood, who by then had something of a fan club among the younger agents, retained his ties with his old organization, and was occasionally given some of their new toys to field test in the woods surrounding his fortress of solitude.

He had become my mentor and friend, solidly so after I introduced him to the Chinese-American beauty and lawyer Elizabeth Sung, who had become a fixture in his cabin, and seemed absolutely devoted to him despite the nearly thirty year difference in their ages.

I told Heather I was bugging out early to pay a visit to Raine. She was concentrating on something on her computer screen and didn't even acknowledge me.

Nine

It was nearing mid-day when I left the office, so I swung by a Burger King and picked up two large double burgers, with fries and shakes. The greasy smell of fries filled the Bug and made my mouth water. Fortunately, the traffic was light, so the drive from the District to River Road, and out to the turnoff to Raine's house, not far from Point of Rocks, only took slightly over an hour. The ice in the drinks was nearly melted, but they're usually so sweet that only makes them taste better to me.

Raine was waiting for me on the porch of his cabin when I pulled up. He had surveillance cameras and sensors in the woods lining the dirt road to his house, but I'd never been able to spot them, even after he showed me the monitors in the small room behind his living room. The ground around the cabin was cleared out to a hundred yards, and inside the cabin he had an arsenal that many small third world countries would pay a ransom for. Anyone trying to sneak up on him was in for a few nasty surprises.

He was nearing eighty, but still stood erect. His hair was now completely white, and he kept it trimmed and brushed neatly, and he was always clean shaven. He normally wore dress slacks and a jacket, even when home alone, but today he was wearing a khaki shirt with pockets on the sleeves and blue denim pants tucked into work boots.

"Hey, young fellow," he said as I got out of the car carrying the bag of food. "Haven't seen you in a long time." He sniffed the air. "I see you made a little detour on the way. Come on in, and I'll set a place at the table."

"I hope you don't mind," I said. "I picked up a little lunch. Burgers okay with you? I know you prefer home cooked food."

He stepped aside and let me enter the cabin. The large room was unchanged from my last visit, with a large sofa in the center, and a large wooden table in front of it. Two stuffed chairs flanked the table. Off to the right was a table big enough for four with four chairs at each side. Behind the sofa was the door to his inner sanctum – the room where he kept his monitoring equipment and armory.

"Burgers are fine," he said. "Lately, Elizabeth has been doing a lot of the cooking, and while I love that woman dearly, her idea of good food is vegetables and tofu. I know it's supposed to be healthy and all, but a man has to have some meat now and then. She absolutely refuses to serve red meat, you know. How is a man supposed to keep his iron levels up without some red meat now and then?"

I put the bag on the table and began removing the contents, setting out one burger and shake for him on the side near the back door, another for me at his right, and piled the fries on the flattened bag in the center.

"This isn't exactly red meat, but it's the best I could do on short notice."

He sat down and grabbed the burger, taking a large bite. He chewed slowly, a look of satisfaction causing his brown face to glow. After swallowing, and then taking a sip of the shake through the straw, he burped and sat back looking at me with a big smile on his face. "It's good enough. Man, I haven't had a hunk of meat in weeks." He picked up one of the little catsup packs and tore it open, squeezing a little mound at the edge of the pile of fries. He thin picked up a fry, dipped it in the catsup, and began eating it slowly, taking little bites and chewing them completely. He ate two fries before turning his attention back to me.

"Hm, that is so good." He unfolded one of the napkins from the bag and wiped daintily at his thin lips. "Now, to what do I owe this unexpected visit in the middle of the day?"

I finished the mouthful of burger I'd taken and, taking another napkin, wiped my own lips – not as daintily as he had. Then, I gave him a quick summary of what I was working on. He continued to demolish the burger and made quite a dent in the fries as I talked. When I finished, he wiped his mouth again and leaned back in his chair.

"Son, it sounds to me like you have yourself two problems." He ticked them off on his long fingers. "One, you got this vermin Coltrane to get rid of. That shouldn't be too hard. Two, you got some force moving in on a community, and using pretty drastic measures to do it – that's a bit more difficult."

Tell me about it, I thought. "So, do you have any suggestions – on dealing with either of them?"

"Sure. This guy Coltrane sounds like a small time hood – actually, more of a poser, since he doesn't even have a record. If you can pin down his movements, where he stashes stuff, and the like, you can just basically pull a double bluff on him. Sounds like he's taking advantage of the timidity of the people in the community, making him a bully in my book, and bullies usually back down when someone badder comes along." He smiled wolfishly at me. "You do know how to be bad, don't you?"

"Well, I don't hold a candle to you, but I think I can be bad enough for Mr. Coltrane."

"Good lad." He laughed. "I have a few gadgets that you might find useful."

He got up and motioned me to follow him to his back room. Inside, he opened the top drawer in a huge cabinet upon which sat his monitoring screens showing the surrounding area in brilliant and well-defined color. A couple of the cameras seemed to be panning slowly from side to side. He pulled two medium sized boxes from the drawer and put them on the top of the cabinet.

Opening one box, he reached in and pulled out four small black objects. They were about two inches by two inches and about an eighth of an inch thick. Made of what looked like some kind of plastic, they had no markings on them. He handed me one. The thing weighed about as much as a deck of cards.

"What is this?" I asked.

"That, son is a bug. State of the art integrated circuitry, built in power supply good for six to eight months without needing a recharge, and has a pickup range of two hundred feet. It transmits its signal over fifty miles over ground and an unlimited distance when it bounces off a satellite." He reached over to a futuristic looking keyboard and tapped a key. "Listen to this," he whispered. *"Listen to this"* came clearly from a small speaker set on the wall near one of the monitors. "See, it can even pick up a whisper."

"Another agency toy they're asking you to test? How am I supposed to get these where they can listen in on Coltrane?"

He held one up in front of my face. "This looks like plastic, and basically it is," he said. "But, it has a small magnet inside. You can easily attach it to any metal surface. I have some double-sided tape you can use to attach it to a wall or ceiling too."

"If I attach this to his car will it pick up conversations from inside the vehicle?"

"Clear as a bell, laddie. And, it turns itself off when there's nothing to listen to. Wouldn't want to waste battery power listening to a car engine, you know. Of course, you'll want to consider this next item when you decide where on the car you want to put it."

He opened the other box and pulled out another deck-of-card sized object. Also black, this one had a row of three LED lights at one end and a circular grille at the other. At the end with the lights there was a bump in the side.

"What the hell is that?" I asked.

"This, my boy is a tracking device. Uses the Global Positioning System to tell you precisely where the person or object it's attached to is, what direction they're moving, and how fast." He tapped another key on the keyboard, pressing the bump on the device at the same time. The centermost monitor flickered and the picture of an area of trees was replaced by a color map with a blinking red dot in the center of the screen. Looking closer, I could see that it was a map of the Maryland-DC area, and the blinking dot was about where we currently were. "Put this on his car, and you can track his movements in real time, anytime using GPS. Just don't put it too close to the bug – they can interfere with each other. Need to be at least twelve inches apart."

I assumed this gizmo also had a magnet in it. "You're letting me borrow these things?"

"I've been thinking about how I would field test them." There was an impish twinkle in his eyes. "This is as good a test as any. I don't have much else to do all day with Elizabeth at her office down in Chinatown. Hell, I was so bored this morning, I was out checking on my monitoring devices in the woods. Not that they need it – I have them placed so even the animals can't disturb them, and the power supplies last forever. This will give me something useful to do."

Now things were looking up. With Blood helping we just might crack this case after all. "Welcome aboard," I said.

Ten

After we had coffee to wash the rest of the burgers and fries down, I put the two boxes in my car and went home.

While I don't normally involve Sandra in my investigations – I still remember how I sweat when the militia kidnapped her and spirited her and Alma off to West Virginia – I couldn't resist showing her Blood's gadgets and discussing with her how I might plant them successfully.

She, however, was more interested in playing with other toys, so the two boxes were left sitting open on my living room floor until I scooped them up the next morning on my way to work.

Before locking the box in the trunk of my

Volkswagen, I took two of the bugs and the GPS tracker and put them in my jacket pocket. They hardly made a budge. I wanted to have them handy in case an opportunity arose to use them.

Heather was waiting for me when I arrived, sitting behind her desk with her coat on and her purse on her lap – a slightly worried look on her face.

"Hey, cheer up, kid," I said, trying to put her at ease. "We'll be in and out of the licensing office in a jiff, trust me."

It didn't really work. She was still looking morose as she slid into the passenger side of my car, and even more so as we found an empty parking slot two blocks from the licensing office on Fourteenth Street.

We'd arrived early, before the rush. There were only five in line ahead of us at the desk where Police Sergeant Melinda Curtis presided. I'd gotten to know her well from my annual visits to get my ticket renewed, and we got along well. At five-eleven and one-fifty, she'd been a street cop until a speeding motorist had clipped her one day when she was writing a ticket for another speeder, breaking her hip. They'd replaced the hip, but she'd never been the same after that, so they'd assigned her to desk duty, and eventually put her in charge of the office that issued licenses to PIs and private security guards. She was good with people, though, always greeting them with a smile on her light brown face and a cheerful twinkle in her dark brown eyes.

When she saw me in line, she adjusted her straightened hair, a lock of which had fallen over her eyes, and gave me an impish wink.

We finally got up to the desk, and I let Heather go first. "Hey, Melinda," I said. "I'd like to introduce you to my partner, Heather Bunche. She's here to apply for her license."

"Hi, hon," she said, beaming at Heather. "Why you lookin' so glum? We don't bite here. You got your fingerprint card and background papers with you?

Heather nodded and took the requested paper from her purse, placing them on the counter. Curtis took a form from a stack at her elbow and placed it on top of the papers.

"Here you go, hon. You just take this form over to the counter there and fill it out and turn it in with your fee, and that's all there is to it."

Heather looked surprised. "That's it? Just fill out the form?"

"That's all there is to it," Curtis said. She looked over Heather's head at me. "You takin' 'em in young ain't you, Al? This child hardly looks twenty-one yet."

"She's older than she looks," I said. "And as tough as nails. I've been teaching her for years."

"Well, if you vouch for her, that's good enough for me. Now, hon, you go on and fill out the form." She took another form from her desk drawer and shoved it toward me. "I already filled out your renewal application, so all you got to do is sign it."

Like I said, I get along with her, and coming in personally makes an impression. Heather gave me a hopeful look as she moved to the counter. We were the only ones left in the office, so I decided to hang about the desk to chat.

"What's been going on with you, Melinda?" I asked as I signed the form and pushed it back to her along with my renewal fee in cash.

She put the form in a neat stack at her right hand and after counting the cash, put it in a green metal box in her right-hand desk drawer. She filled out a receipt and handed it to me. "Same-O, same-o," she said. "I sit here every day wishin' I could get back out on the streets."

"They still won't clear you for street

duty?"

"Naw - the hip done healed, but the doctors say it's still prone to breakin' if I put too much stress on it, so the department won't take no chances. They gone have to give me disability when I retire anyway, but if I break my hip again, they'd have to pay a hundred percent, and I might not be able to walk right."

"That's too bad. You were a good street cop." I knew how it must have rankled her to be confined to a desk. Buster knew her and he'd described her as one of the toughest cops on the force, male or female. She'd been the terror of many a street hustler and mugger in her day. Keeping her inside was like putting a race horse out to pasture.

"Yeah, I liked it out on the street," she said. "But, you gotta play the cards you're dealt. Don't much matter now, though – I'm retirin' in a coupla years. Hey, maybe when I retire I'll become a PI like you. You thinkin' 'bout expandin' that business of yours?"

She seemed serious. But, she was talking two years in the future, and I'd been operating from day to day. "I haven't given it much thought really," I said. "But, in two years – who knows. Give me a call when you retire."

"I'm gone do that, you know. By the way,

I'm gettin' married in a few weeks, too. How 'bout that?"

"You – married?" I didn't even know she had a boyfriend. Of course, the subject had never come up in our casual conversations. I think I'd been assuming she was already married. "Congratulations."

She must have sensed what I was thinking. "I know you surprised," she said. "Nobody ever figure a big broad like me can find a man. We been seein' each other for two years now, but last week he finally popped the question. I guess he want me to make him an honest man."

She held up her hand to show off her engagement ring. A white gold number with a stone the size of a garbanzo bean – it gleamed in the light from the overhead fixtures.

Just then, Heather came up and put her completed form on the desk. Her eyes lit up at the sight of the ring.

"Wow – that's a beautiful ring," she said. "You're a lucky woman to have someone give you something like that."

Curtis's brown cheeks flamed red, and she smiled shyly as she held the ring up for Heather to take a closer look. "Don't I know it," she said. "It ain't the real thing of course, but it's the thought that counts. My man got it from one of the street dealers over in Anacostia – one of Deacon Coltrane's boys. It's just cubic zirconium, but I love it anyway. He got a good deal on it 'cause he's Deacon's second cousin, you know, and Deacon runs some kind of shopping network. He sells all kind of things to people over the phone, including these phony diamond rings. He let my man have this one as a kind of wedding present. Ain't it pretty?"

Heather looked at me and frowned. I perked up at the sound of Coltrane's name.

"Coltrane deals in jewelry?" I asked.

"Oh yeah; the Deacon he a fixture over in Anacostia for a long time now. He deal in just 'bout everything – junk jewelry, appliances, gold coins. He even do some real estate from time to time. I think he get stuff from them distributors up in New York and New Jersey – you know - them folk what advertise on TV. He must get it wholesale, 'cause he sell it for less than they charge on TV. You know him?"

"No – I met him once, but he didn't mention anything about his business." I saw an opening to get at Coltrane. "Say, I've been thinking about buying a birthday present for my girlfriend. You think he could make me a good deal for a bracelet or necklace?"

"If Deacon can't get it for you it can't be got. You oughta go over and see him."

I told her I'd do that and asked for directions. She wrote an Anacostia address on a little yellow sticky note and handed it to me. After some more mutual gushing over her ring, Heather paid her fee, and she gave us slips with instructions to take them to a room down the hall from hers where we would be photographed and issued our laminated licenses.

That process took twenty minutes and in just over an hour we were back at the car, me with another year on my ticket, and Heather the proud possessor of a brand new private eye license. She was beaming like a kid at Christmas as the wrap comes off that American Flyer bike she's always wanted.

She beamed most of the way back to the office, occasionally taking the license out of her wallet and looking at it.

"Well, kid," I said. "It's official now. You're a full partner."

"Wow!" was all she could say.

She was silent for a moment, and then a frown crossed her face.

"What's the problem?" I asked.

"I just remembered something," she said. "That sergeant – she said her ring was cubic zirconium, didn't she?"

"Yeah, I doubt her fiancé could afford a real diamond unless he stole one, and Coltrane might be an angel like that article said, but I don't see him giving a real diamond away, not even to his cousin."

"Well, I'm no expert, but I do know diamonds, and that stone she's wearing is *not* a cubic zirconium."

Now it was my turn to look stunned. "What?"

"That was a real diamond in that ring, and from the size, I'd say it was at least one full carat."

"She said Coltrane dealt in paste - cheap junk jewelry. Where would he get his hands on a one carat diamond?"

"Where indeed?"

"Looks like Mr. Coltrane and I will have some interesting things to discuss when I visit him this afternoon," I said. "When we get back to the office I want you to run his background again, and I want you to dig *deep*. There's more to this guy than meets the eye."

Death and Taxis

Eleven

Deacon Coltrane's base of operations was in a two-story, red brick building that looked from the outside like an abandoned warehouse. It was located near the intersection of Twenty-Second and R Streets just south of the Sousa Bridge over the Anacostia River. The building didn't have a sign outside. I guessed that since Coltrane's business was mostly by phone, he figured there was no need to advertise his physical location.

The area was what I remembered from a previous visit – depressed and desperate. Lots of weed-strewn vacant lots littered with trash, graffiti on the sides of most buildings of the type you didn't repeat in polite company, and dour looking men in faded pants lounging about on street corners engaged in animated conversations about nothing in particular.

It wasn't what I would have expected from Coltrane. He'd impressed me as someone for whom appearances were everything. I would have thought he'd be operating out of a gleaming glass, steel, and concrete edifice with a sign out front in gold lettering. Instead, the building was stained black and gray from years of pollution, with green mold growing in gaps between the bricks, and rust holes in the drain pipes. In a couple of places on the ground floor, broken window panes had been covered with sheetrock rather than being replaced, giving the building a derelict look. It wasn't what I would have expected from a man who was allegedly raking in the kind of money Coltrane was.

In addition to the older men, many of whom looked past their working prime, and probably getting by on social security or disability checks, there were a few younger looking men – boys – hanging about. Something in the way they lounged told me they weren't as inattentive or idle as first appearances might indicate. Whether it's a jungle or a street corner, a sentry is a sentry. I could tell lookouts when I saw them. I would have bet money that under their baggy NFL team jackets they were carrying something other than wallets.

A large lot on the right side of the

building, with Coltrane's purple Cadillac and four or five other expensive looking cars, was obviously the facility's parking lot. None of the kids doing lookout duty on the sidewalk seemed to be paying any attention to the parking lot. I mentally tossed a coin, and decided against parking on the street. I'd take my chances that if I parked in the lot and was challenged, I'd bluff my way by flashing my PI license. No one challenged me as I turned into the lot from the street. I nosed up against the building, a few cars away from the pimp mobile. Then, I remembered the 'Police Business' placard I'd 'borrowed' from Buster. I took it out of the glove apartment and placed it on the dash.

I got out of the Volkswagen and looked around. No one seemed to be noticing me. Casually, I walked toward the Cadillac. When I reached it, I eased toward the passenger side and knelt. I quickly slipped the transmitter from my pocket and slid it under the passenger-side door, slapping it against a flat metal surface. Without standing, I eased toward the rear and repeated the procedure with the GPS tracker, putting it under the back behind the wheel well. I looked around to make sure no one had noticed, and then stood, brushing off my jacket and walked on to the front of the building.

I bumped into one of the young 'sentries' as I came around the corner.

"What you doin' back here?" he asked, glaring at me with bloodshot eyes. "This lot for people that work here. You gone have to move yo car."

I eased my PI license from my pocket and held it in front of his pimply face. "I guess you could say I'm temporarily working here now," I said. "I have business with Mr. Coltrane."

"You don't work here, you s'posed to park on the street."

The kid was a foot shorter than me, and must have weighed in at one-thirty. I leaned down until my face was just inches from his. His breath was like sweaty gym socks, causing me to breathe through my mouth and hope whatever he had wasn't airborne. "You planning to watch my car for me while I'm inside?"

"Uh, Deacon don't pay me to watch no cars."

"Well, he and I have important business. What do you think he'll say if I tell him I had to leave my car where it might get stolen?"

He blinked his bloodshot eyes. My question had strained the few synapses in his brain that were still working, but he understood the implication – he might be just about to piss off someone connected to the man who paid him. He didn't need a PhD to know that wasn't a good idea.

"Okay," he said. "I guess it okay you park there."

He turned and went back to his post on the sidewalk.

When I first joined the army, a sergeant told me the way to keep people off your back was to look like you were busy. His way was to walk around with a clipboard under his arm and look as if he was inspecting things. The corollary on the street is to talk and act as if you're the meanest, baddest dude around – so bad, in fact, you don't even have to threaten and bluster. You stare people in the eye and basically dare them to stand in your way. It works ninety percent of the time – you have to be prepared for fight or flight the other ten percent. This time, it fell well within the ninety percent.

I was almost whistling to myself as I pushed open the rusty metal door and entered the building.

I wasn't sure what I'd been expecting, but what I got was a complete shock.

The interior of the building had about as much relationship with its exterior and surroundings as a BMW parked in a tin-roofed shed. It didn't look like the digs of a wealthy businessman from the outside, but inside, it was all business, and looked lucrative.

It was a large cavernous space, with walls painted in a neutral beige, beige carpeting on the floor, and white, soundproofing tiles in the ceiling. A six-foot wide aisle ran down the center and to each side was a series of cubicles with four-foot high beige walls, topped by glass walls that ran up to over six feet. A narrow cross passage ran off from the main aisle between each set of two cubicles. I counted forty cubicles on each side, inside of which forty people, men and women of various ages, black, white, Asian, and Hispanic, sat wearing headphones and murmuring into telephone speakers. In the background, soft music came from hidden speakers. Along the walls were large posters with inspirational quotations and fancy photographs of mountains and soaring eagles.

None of the workers paid any attention to me as I made my way down the center aisle toward a glass walled office in the back.

Delmar Coltrane, dressed in a metallic gray suit, pink tie, and powder blue shirt, sat behind a massive wooden desk watching me approach. As I neared the door, he reached under the desk, and the door swung open.

"Come in, Mr. Pennyback," he said as I entered. "What can I do for you today?"

Like any good businessman, he was good at remembering names, and he didn't seem to be affected by the tone of our first meeting.

He was still dressed like a pimp, but his manner was that of a high-powered businessman, even if there was a hint of the street in his speech, and his office matched. The side and back walls were light mahogany, and covered with pictures of him with various local notables, and certificates from a number of well-known local civic organizations. A large gray steel safe sat against the wall behind him. He motioned me to a cushioned chair at the right front edge of his desk.

"I was told that you're the man to see if I need a present for a special person," I said as I eased myself into the chair.

"Well now, I guess you was told right," he said. "What kinda present you got in mind?"

"That's my problem. The person I want it for is kind of hard to please – you know how women can be. Maybe if you'd give me some idea of what kind of merchandise you have, I'd think of something."

His brown face lit up in a predatory smile. "I know what you talkin' 'bout, brother man.

Women always hard to please, but you come to the right place. You name it, and I got it – from diamond bracelets to vacuum cleaners – something to please every woman."

He was looking at me like I was a Christmas goose ready for plucking, so I thought I'd keep playing along.

"Uh, well, I don't know about diamonds," I said. "I'm not exactly rolling in money, and she's not the domestic type, so I don't think she'd like a vacuum cleaner."

Playing the bewildered boyfriend, I shoved my hands into my jacket pockets and leaned forward. I grasped the remaining bug and palmed it. Coltrane seemed to be taking in my act, if the gleam in his eyes was any indication.

"Hey, bro, no problem. The diamonds I sell ain't the real thing. They them, what you call 'em – cubic zirconium. Look like the real thing, but a lot cheaper, you know what I'm talkin' 'bout?"

I used my thumbnail to start peeling back the plastic covering the adhesive on the device. When I felt I had uncovered enough to allow it to adhere, I eased my hands from my pocket, but continued to lean forward. I put my hands between my legs. "Well, I don't know," I said. "She might not appreciate me giving her a diamond that wasn't real."

I eased the device under the chair, affixing it to the back of the front rail.

"So, this chick of yours be the fussy type, huh?" He closed one eye and looked at me with his head cocked to one side. "Well, I just might be able to help you, you know. I done got my hands on a few real rocks – primo stones – I might be able to cut you a deal for one."

"What kind of deal, and for what size stone?"

He made a circle with his thumb and forefinger. Roughly the same size as the stone Melinda Curtis was wearing. "I can let you have one like that for . . . say . . . two grand?"

"Wow," I said, leaning back in the chair. "I don't have that kind of money. My business eats up most of what I make." That was a lie, but he was eating it up. I was getting his measure – Coltrane was a con man, and if I made him think I was desperate, he might expose more of himself.

"No problem, bro – I can cut you a deal. Arrange installment payments. It only cost you five percent interest."

"That makes the total cost twenty-one hundred. I don't know – I might be able to swing it. It'd take me a couple of months, though."

Now, it was his turn to lean back in his chair. "No, brother man," he said. "Not a flat five percent. I mean five percent a week." He waved his hands. "But, that still be a better deal than you get at one of them jewelry stores in town."

"I . . . don't know . . . I'll have to think about it. You got anything else she might like?"

"Not knowin' the chick, that's hard to say, bro. I mean, I got timeshares, gold coins – all kinds of shit. She's your woman, you oughta know what she like and don't like."

He was right about that. I did know what Sandra liked, and I doubt if his fake diamonds, or even the real ones, which were likely hot, would impress her. I didn't think I'd get any more out of him. Like most con men, he was more interested in pumping me for information than divulging things about himself. But, I'd at least managed to do what I came for – I'd bugged his office and car, and with Blood monitoring, I'd know where he went. So, I decided to break it off and get the hell out of his presence before I let how I really felt about him show.

"I get you," I said. "I guess I'll have to think about this some more. How about I come back in a few days after I figure out what she wants, and what I can afford?"

"You do that, bro," he said. "I ain't goin' nowhere."

He never asked me what kind of business I was in. But, I had no doubt he'd find out. He had that gleam in his eyes of someone who's spotted a sucker and he was planning to reel me in.

Twelve

On the way back to the office I got an attack of the munchies so bad I could hear my stomach growling over the sound of the engine. I pulled into a Popeye's and ordered their spicy Cajun chicken special. I was just pulling the crispy meat from my second leg when my cell phone rang. It was Blood.

"Hey, son," he said. "The bug you planted in Coltrane's office has already produced results. You might want to come out here and listen to the tape."

I don't rush my fried chicken. I finished the meal, ordered one to go, called Heather to let her know I'd be coming back late, and headed across town to Blood's place. He was waiting for me on his front porch.

"Wish you'd brought me some of that chicken," he said as I got out of the car –

then his face beamed as he saw the bag I was holding.

"Way ahead of you, partner."

He almost snatched the bag from my hand. "Now, that's a lunch for a man." He took a deep breath. "That aroma brings back memories of my childhood."

"You gonna eat first, or tell me why I had to drive all the way out here?"

"Oh, yes." He shook himself out of his food-induced reverie. "I reckon the chicken can wait. Come on back to my control room. I have something you need to hear."

He dropped the bag on the table as we passed and went back to the rear room. He sat in a leather backed chair at the monitor table and motioned me to its companion. After a few stabs at the keyboard, the sound of hissing static came from speakers I couldn't see. Then, the static clarified into words – the volume wasn't very high, but it was perfectly intelligible.

"Billy, get yo ass in here." I heard Coltrane's voice.

"What you want, boss?"

There was the crackling sound of papers being shuffled.

"You see that dude was just in here?"

"Yeah, won't he the one was at the funeral the other day?"

"That's him. He come here sayin' he want to buy his bitch a present."

"So, lots of people do that, boss."

"Yeah, but he ask a lot of questions, and he don't buy nothin', you dig. I think he up to somethin'."

"What that be, boss?"

"Damn, nigger – if I knew that I wouldn't be settin' here talkin' 'bout it, now would I?"

"What you want me to do, boss?"

For several seconds there was silence except for muffled scuffling sounds.

"I wants you to check him out, that's what. Find out what he up to."

"You think he know what you been doin'?"

"No. If he did, he wouldn't have just been sittin' here askin' me questions. I think he might suspect, though, or maybe he just fishin'. That what I want you to find out."

"What you want me to do if he know somethin'?"

"Now, come on, Billy boy – I ain't got to tell

you that. You knows what you got to do. Now get your ass out there and find out what he up to. I'm gone go check on my other operations."

More scuffling and the sound of muffled footsteps, and then silence.

"That's it for now," Raine said. "He must still be in the building, though, because the GPS shows his car hasn't moved, and there's been no sound from the bug you put there."

"The building does have a second floor," I said. "I didn't get a look at that. I wonder what his other operations are."

"You might do better by wondering what this Billy character will do when he finds out you're snooping around their operations – speaking of which, just what is it this guy does?"

Looked like some kind of telemarketing operation to me." I described what I'd seen and what Coltrane had told me about his business.

Blood shook his head. "Sounds more like a boiler room to me."

"A what?"

"A boiler room," he said. "That's a big scam operation designed to part gullible people from their money. He might even be doing some legitimate marketing on the side just in case the authorities come snooping around, but I'll bet mostly he's selling time shares, real estate, coins, and other so-called moneymaking items – all of which are over-priced and/or phony."

"You mean this dude's bilking poor people of their money?" I asked incredulously.

"With the phony jewelry, maybe – but, no, these scams go after people who have money. Usually the elderly, and mostly men because they tend to be more insecure and vulnerable to scams. You ever have someone call and offer to let you in on the ground floor of a great real estate deal?"

"No, and I doubt I'd listen to such a call," I said. "If it's all that great, why would someone call and offer it to me instead of taking it himself?"

"If more people asked that question scams like this would be far less effective," he said, chuckling. "You don't know too much about con artists, do you, son?"

"Well, I remember the old Birmingham bus station scam from back in the 60s, when some dude would come up and ask you to hold some money for him, and you'd end up taking out your wallet, and before you knew it, he'd be gone with all your cash."

He laughed and patted me on the arm.

"Boy, you are totally out of it. The cons that get run today make a gyp like that bush league. Nowadays, they got people who contact you by phone and sell you oil leases – only the well, if they even have one, is just a dry hole. They'll sell you gold coins at markups up to five hundred percent. You get a box of coins that when you try to sell later you'd be lucky to get a nickel on every dollar you spent. Hell, they even use TV commercials – get some washed up star to shill for some moneymaking deal like prepaid phone card machines. They claim you can make thirty or forty thousand bucks a year, but you'd have to live to be a hundred to make back what you pay for the damn thing. Some of these guys pull down millions every year with these scams."

"Who the hell falls for deals like that?" I asked.

"You'd be surprised. Doctors, lawyers, even college professors get gyped every day. These guys especially like to go after older people. If you got money, and you let your feelings and emotions get mixed up in your financial decisions, you're ripe for the picking. They specialize in playing on fear and insecurity – people looking to make a quick buck, guys down on their luck and looking for a way out."

"Seems to me anyone would ask a few

questions before parting with their money like that."

"Hell, if you start asking a con man questions about his so-called deal, he'll cut you off and go looking for another sucker. That might be why your friend Coltrane's a bit leery about you. I didn't play the part of the tape from when you were in his office, but you *did* ask a lot of questions that would raise alarm bells for any con man."

"Well, I did ask him a few questions about the stuff he claims he's selling, but isn't that normal?"

"Not for a scam artist. You start asking questions rather than answering his questions, and warning bells go off in his head. These guys like to manipulate people – and people who ask questions are harder to manipulate. That means you're thinking, and they don't want you to think."

Shit. That closed off that avenue to get at Coltrane. There were a lot of things I guess I didn't know. At least I'd planted the devices, so we could keep track of him.

"Well, I guess I might just have to confront him directly to get him to lay off Nkrumah and his people," I said.

"That might work, but be careful," Blood said. "A lot of these guys are addicts – hooked on one substance or another, and you can never tell what a junkie might do. He's likely to have a lot of drug users working for him as well."

"You think he might be dealing drugs?"

He shrugged. "Hard to say. He's likely to do anything that makes money. I said he might be a user. He could just be greedy. Most con artists get started early in life – scamming people when they're kids – and it becomes a habit that's as hard to break as drugs. Some do it for the rush a successful con gives them. I'd have to see this Coltrane character for myself to tell which he is. Maybe monitoring his conversations for a few days I'll be able to get a fix on him. In the meantime, I think you have that bigger problem – what do you plan to do about whoever's killing the cab drivers?"

"I don't have a clue. I've got Heather trying to piece together the dead drivers' movements just before they were killed to see if I can find something that ties them together. Buster's looking into gang activity to see if there are any clues there. Until we know more, I'm just treading water."

"Well, if you need my help on that, you know where to find me. Now, if you don't mind, I'm going to get me a taste of that chicken before the grease on it congeals."

Charles Ray

Death and Taxis

Thirteen

It was after two when I left Blood demolishing the last of the spicy chicken, trying to get it eaten and the evidence destroyed before Elizabeth got home. He was becoming almost henpecked, but I sensed he enjoyed his status. When I met him he'd been living alone for a long time. After I introduced him to Elizabeth, and she decided to move in, I'd noticed a few subtle changes in his behavior – he was smiling more for one thing.

I toyed with the idea of going home, but figured since it was Heather's first day as a real PI I'd help her close up for a change.

I didn't get back to the office until after three, not leaving time for much real work – but enough time for Heather to drop a bomb on me.

"I haven't heard back from the cab

companies yet on the call sheets," she said as I walked in. "But, I did pick up something on the cabbie that was killed yesterday. A friend of mine at Justice who has a friend in fraud and white collar crime said they'd been watching him. Apparently he had international connections from his home country and was helping them smuggle diamonds into the area."

I stopped in the act of removing my jacket, my mouth agape.

"You mean like blood diamonds?"

"No, not diamonds from West Africa," she said. "Apparently, this guy was working with South Africans and Israelis to smuggle diamonds from his home country, Zimbabwe. They have alluvial diamonds there – that's the kind that are just below the surface, and according to my contact, they're first rate gemstones. The government there is so corrupt, it's easy for people to smuggle the stones out of the country, mainly to South Africa where they sell them to larger smuggling operations for movement to Europe and North America. It's all very confusing, but my friend said they were hoping he would lead them to his international contacts. Unfortunately, he was killed before he could do that."

If the feds had their oars in the water

things could get muddied real fast. There is no love lost between local cops and federal agents. Often, outfits like the FBI and DEA will keep information from their local counterparts for bureaucratic reasons, and in retaliation, locals sometimes fail to share everything they know. When you have different crimes being committed by the same individual, it can be a nightmare trying to figure out who knows what. My guess was the feds hadn't shared their information with DC metro, and since murder is under local jurisdiction, the DC cops probably hadn't even thought to check with their federal friends. That left Heather and me to navigate between the two – not an enviable position to be in. It would be tough to just sort out which federal agency had primary jurisdiction. I could just imagine the tangle as Customs, the FBI, and Treasury, to name a few, wrestled with which one of them had lead. Hell, if any of the smuggling was being done by ship, even the Coast Guard would be involved.

"Do the feds think his murder was related to his smuggling activity?" I asked.

"My friend wasn't sure," she said. She shrugged. "She said they're still processing it."

Meaning they were arguing over who dropped the ball most likely. The one thing the feds are good at is dodging the blame when things go wrong.

"Well, keep digging. In the meantime, I think I'd better let Buster know."

He wasn't going to be happy.

Fourteen

To say that Buster was pissed at the news would be the understatement of the century. After I told him what we'd learned, he pounded the table so hard, Mom rushed over to see if something was wrong. He apologized for his outburst, placating her – she was so happy to see us for the second time in the same day, she was more than accommodating. Buster had a ham sandwich, home fries and cup coffee in front of him. I'd just ordered coffee.

"Fuckin' feds got one of my CIs under surveillance, and they don't even have the decency to let me know," he said when she was out of earshot. "I wonder how many others they lookin' at we don't know 'bout?"

All I could do was look sympathetic. "The real question is, could his involvement in a smuggling operation have anything to do with his murder, and how does that relate to the others," I said. I didn't bother reminding him that federal authorities didn't have to notify local police about their investigations – national security, need-to-know, and all that.

"Hell," he said. "Who knows? Some of these smuggling outfits are as vicious as drug gangs, and diamonds – man, talk about low overhead, high return. Guy can bring in a few million worth of stones in his pocket, and if he don't trigger a close inspection at the airport, he's home free. For that kind of cash, some people might do anything. Shit, if there's a jewelry smuggling operation going on here using cab drivers, who the hell knows? What I don't understand is why use drivers in the first place when they could just put a bunch of diamonds in some dude's pocket, and let him walk through the airport with 'em"?

The angrier Buster got the less of the ghetto was apparent in his speech. When he was really steamed, he sounded more like a college professor than a smart-mouth, street savvy cop. He could make the change anytime he chose – which is what made him such a good cop; he was equally at home with the upper crust as with the bros in the hood – but, when he was upset, he reverted back to his middle class, college-educated roots.

"If smuggling is the cause, how does that relate to efforts to move into the African immigrant community?"

"Well, it for damn sure can't be looking for customers," he said. "Most of these people are struggling to just get by. Maybe they're looking for ways to pass the stones, or recruiting mules, or . . . hell, I don't know. It makes no sense."

I shook my head. "The one thing that *is* true," I said. "Is that it makes no sense. We have to check it out, but there's something fishy about it. Why would diamond smugglers be interested in a working class community, for instance?"

"Remember the dudes who were trying to hide their terrorist cell in the community last year?" he said. "Maybe this is a bunch of Africans trying to find a place to set up headquarters where they won't be noticed."

"Not likely. Heather's friend said the dead driver was working with South Africans and Israelis. I can't see either being exactly welcomed in the African community, and they'd stand out like neon signs, even here in DC."

"Assuming you mean a white South African," he said, laughing. "*Especially* here in DC. Okay, so that's not the reason. What does that leave us with?"

"That, my friend, leave us with bupkis." Actually, it left us with less than nothing. If this involved international smuggling and a federal investigation, it would effectively freeze Buster out, and was a bit beyond where I was willing to go, considering I was doing it for free.

Buster slammed his fist into the table again – a bit quieter this time to avoid incurring Mom's wrath. "No, dammit. I'm not letting the feds keep me from getting to the bottom of this." He shot me a pleading look. "You're not gonna bail on me, are you, bro?"

I don't bail on friends. He knew it without asking, but the fact that he felt he had to ask showed how frustrated – and desperate – he was. Buster's that kind of cop. For many, a confidential informant is just a resource, a disposable resource at that. To him, they were human beings who were putting their trust in him, and in some cases their lives on the line. When something happened to them, he took it seriously. I could relate to that.

"No way am I bailing," I said. "But, what do we do about the feds. You already have this turkey Helsing on your ass; now you want a bunch suits from Uncle Sam giving you shit as well? Interfering in a federal investigation is a pretty serious matter."

"Murder's a pretty serious matter. Seven

guys, three that worked for me, had their throats laid open and were left to bleed out in their cars. You think I give a rat's ass about Uncle Sam not getting a little customs duty on a few smuggled diamonds, which are probably gonna be bought by some politician's wife anyway, when we got somebody running around my city killing *my* people? Helsing and the feds think I'm gonna roll over and take this; they can kiss my ass, because I. Will. Not. Do. It."

There it was. Buster Mayweather and Al Pennyback were going to war against the Metro police, the feds, and an as yet to be identified gang that liked to kill people. The odds were completely stacked against us. But, right was on our side. Buster hit it dead on – in the greater scheme of things, while smuggling is a crime, murder is a worse crime. If Helsing and the feds wanted to pursue their bureaucratic agendas and ignore that fact, too bad for them.

We were going to kick ass and take names.

Fifteen

The first ass I planned to kick belonged to one Delmar 'Deacon' Coltrane. The Deacon was a minor irritant that I'd let hang about far too long, and he was interfering with the important operation – identifying whoever it was that was killing Buster's informants.

Coltrane would be my early Christmas present to Joseph Nkrumah and his community. Sending him scurrying back into the dark recesses of the ghetto where he belonged, where he could operate his little boiler room scam among his own kind, was, as I saw it, just a bit of community service.

I was sitting in my office the next morning, staring at a blank computer screen and going over in my mind the best way to do a bit of pest control when the light on my phone started blinking.

"Yeah, kid," I said. "What is it?"

"It's Mr. Nkrumah on the line for you, Al," Heather said.

I had her put him through. "Yes, Mr. Nkrumah, what can I do for you?"

"Mr. Pennyback," he said in his clipped British accent. "Mr. Coltrane just called me. He is coming to talk to me about his proposal to establish himself as a partner in the businesses in the community. I would be most grateful if you could be here as well."

Problem solved. I'd been toying with the idea of bearding the lion in his den, but if he was going hunting, it would be even better to confront him away from all his goons. He'd probably just have the big gorilla that drove for him – not a real problem. I told Nkrumah I'd be there in thirty minutes.

I was there in twenty. Coltrane hadn't arrived.

"What time did he say he was coming?" I asked.

Nkrumah had a worried look on his face. He was tapping his fingers on a worn Bible he had on the desk in his cramped office, a little cubicle above a tailor shop, whose walls were lined with posters advertising the services available to new immigrants. The place had a smell of oil and peanuts, and was in need of a good dusting. I figured Nkrumah couldn't afford custodial services, and was too busy with his community organizing activities to clean the place himself. He could also have used the services of a good administrative assistant. His desk was strewn with papers, forms, and brochures, and crumpled bags from local take-out restaurants were overflowing from the dented metal waste can at the corner of the desk. Heather would freak if she ever saw the place.

"He only said he was on his way. I assumed he would arrive before you did."

Just as well. It might throw him off stride to see me there ahead of him. I sat on a metal folding chair off to the side and picked up a magazine from a stack of periodicals printed in various African countries. This one was about the wildlife parks of the continent. It had some outstanding wildlife photography, and pictures of wealthy white tourists being shown the richness of Africa by well-dressed, well-dressed guides. Everyone in the photos was smiling. I'd never been to Africa, but I'd met quite a few of the immigrants in the Washington area, and from their stories, I doubted if any of them had ever been photographed for this particular magazine. As I idly leafed through the pages, Nkrumah busied himself with a stack of papers on his desk, glancing nervously up at the door every few minutes.

The minutes ticked by. I can go for long periods of silence; a legacy of many recon patrols where talking could get you killed. But, it seemed a good chance to get to know Nkrumah better – and, to get to know his community better. It might give me some clues as to who was trying to move in on them – besides Coltrane.

I cleared my throat. Nkrumah looked up at me. "Nkrumah," I said. "That's a name from Ghana, right?"

"Uh, yes, it is. I see you're familiar with Africa's history. Nkrumah was the name of my country's first post-independence president – Kwame Nkrumah. Alas, like him, Nkrumah is not the name I was born with. He was born Francis Nwia Kofi Ngonloma, which I think you will agree is quite a mouthful, even for an African. Kwame Nkrumah was the revolutionary name he adopted; for you see, he was, in addition to being an ardent pan-African and nationalist, a committed Marxist." He rubbed at the gray stubble just visible on his broad lower jaw as he spoke, his eyes staring off into the middle distance. "I am from the Gurma tribe, one of Ghana's smaller tribes, far smaller than the dominant Ashanti. My father was a successful merchant, though, who was able to prosper under President Nkrumah, even as the country was descending into economic chaos.

He pushed the papers he'd been reading aside, now fully immersed in his story.

"I was sent here to this country to attend college just before Nkrumah was overthrown and forced into exile in Guinea. It was, I recall, my last year of graduate study at Howard when Flight Lieutenant Jerry John Rawlings" He pronounced it 'lef-tenant.' "overthrew the military government that had ousted Nkrumah. I mistakenly assumed it would be safe to return home. Memories, though, were long. Many people suffered under Nkrumah's misguided attempt to bring socialism to Ghana, and those who were seen to be a part of that suffering were marked. I was forced to change my name and flee the country. I made it back here in 1991, thanks to the efforts to some of my former professors."

"Having changed your name," I said. "That must have been difficult."

"Actually, it was not. At that time, this government was a bit disillusioned with Rawlings, so I was able to apply for asylum. The immigration authorities were very understanding about my need to use an alias, so they admitted me provided I got a legal name change in the courts. Five years later, I applied for citizenship under my new name – forever ridding myself of the past. I have since dedicated myself to helping others new to this country make their way as I have been able to. It is my small way of paying back those who helped me."

"So, in all that time you've had no contact with people back home?"

His dark brown eyes glistened. "There is no one to contact," he said. "My mother died a few months after I returned, and my father was killed by a group of vigilantes. I had no brothers or sisters, and the few cousins would not want to be associated with me. No, Mr. Pennyback, this is now my home."

I could see the hurt in his eyes, though. Washington might be his home, but there would always be a hole in his heart for the home he'd been forced to leave behind. I decided to change the subject. "Tell me, Mr. Nkrumah, just why do you think Coltrane is so anxious to insert himself into your community?"

"Please call me Joseph." There was gratitude in his expression for the chance to talk – and think – about another subject. "You must understand, Mr. Pennyback; while most of our people are not individually wealthy, they are very tribal, clan, and family oriented. In those groupings there is economic power. A family of ten or twelve can marshal a significant bit of capital. That is how many of our businesses were started – everyone in the family pools their resources for one to start the business. He then puts money back into the family to give the next person a chance."

What he was describing was common in Asia as well. A practice that many non-immigrant groups don't seem to understand – from urban black ghetto to white Appalachian shanty town – Americans are so obsessed with the individual, group activity is hard to organize. The immigrants, on the other hand, know the power of the group, and are willing to subordinate individual desires to help the group as a whole prosper. Unfortunately, that often disappears among the first generation born in the U.S., who adopts the 'me-focus of our consumer culture whole hog. So, Coltrane was trying to tap into that community dynamic.

"I see; Coltrane wants to come in and take advantage of already established businesses without having helped get them going."

"Oh, it is far more than that. If he merely wanted to invest, and was willing to pay a fair price, there would not be much of a problem. He wants to change the way our people do business – bring in the cheap merchandise he sells over the phone, use our businesses as a conduits for his other operations such as real estate. He would disrupt the fabric of our community, which we have spent so much time and effort to build."

"I guess I'll have to convince him that this is not a good place to invest," I said.

He looked at me with a puzzled expression on his face. "I have tried for weeks now to do precisely that. How do you hope to achieve it?"

"By appealing to his sense of self preservation," I said simply.

He continued to give me that puzzled look until the meaning of what I'd said penetrated, and then it turned to a slightly disapproving frown. I could understand that. He and most of his community had come from countries where force and intimidation were the tools of first choice. Here in America, they had been able to live under a system that more or less respected the rule of law. But, in poor communities, the law sometimes doesn't reach too often or effectively, and the law of the jungle rules. Under those circumstances, when you're being attacked by a big dog, sometimes the best you can do is get a bigger dog.

I could see that he was contemplating my meaning, and it wasn't pleasing, and that I could understand. He'd probably seen more than his share of violence.

"I would like to be able to settle this matter peacefully," he said finally. "Most of my people have come here to escape violence. I would not like to reintroduce it into their lives."

So, for that matter, would I. But, I believe in being straight with people, and there was no way I could make such a promise. I had no control over Coltrane's reaction. I had him figured for a bully, and hoped that a direct confrontation would be as distasteful to him as it obviously was to Nkrumah. All the same, the choice was his to make. If he wanted his community free of Coltrane's intrusion, he might have to close his eyes to my methods. I decided to give it to him directly.

"I can't promise that. I'm hoping he'll be reasonable, but if he isn't it could get a bit ugly. It's your call."

Walking away and letting a predator like Coltrane nibble away at the fabric of a hard working bunch of people like this would gnaw at me, but I'd swallow that pill if that's the way he wanted it. It wasn't like he was paying me to solve his problem.

Nkrumah, though, was practical and dedicated to his people. The anguish was clear in his eyes, but there was fire there as well. He knew he had to do what was necessary or he risked seeing everything he and his people had worked so hard for destroyed. He took a deep breath and looked at me. He wasn't happy about it, but he was a dedicated man who realized that some sacrifice had to be made for the greater good. "Very well. Do what you must."

As if on cue there was a clomping sound on the stairs leading up to his office, and after a few seconds the door was shoved open with a bang. Coltrane, followed by his hulking driver, stood in the door, a smug look on his face until he spied me sitting in the corner, then his lips turned down in a frown and his eyes narrowed suspiciously. He took a few seconds to regain his composure, and I'll give him credit, he almost managed to ignore me.

"Mr. Nkrumah," he said. "I come to give you one last chance to talk some sense into your people up here."

Nkrumah remained seated – a sure sign of his contempt for Coltrane, who didn't seem to notice or care. The big brute that drove for him squeezed past him into the room, filling the remaining space with his presence.

"I have told you many times already, Mr. Coltrane," Nkrumah said. "Your participation in our businesses is not acceptable to my people."

Coltrane took the four steps across the room to the desk, and then moved to the edge, away from me. I noticed that even though he spoke to Nkrumah, he watched me out of the corner of his eye. I sat as immobile as a statue, looking from him to his goon who glared back at me.

"Look," Coltrane said. "What you people got against makin' money? I'm offerin' you a deal you ain't gone get from nobody else."

"Fifty percent ownership of a business that a family has struggled to build is hardly a good deal," Nkrumah said, his voice dripping with derision.

"Okay, maybe that's too much." Coltrane held his hands out, palms down. He turned up the wattage on his smile. "I ain't greedy. How 'bout twenty-five percent, and I pay top dollar. I just ask they carry my line of products, you dig."

"That is still unacceptable."

"Man, you drive a hard bargain. I come up here offerin' to make you and your people rich, and you blow me off. You Africans is strange people. Okay, what is acceptable?"

I leaned forward. "I think that Mr. Nkrumah is trying to say that the only acceptable condition is for you and your lap dog to leave," I said. "And, don't let the door hit you in the ass on the way out."

Some of the voltage went out of his smile as he turned to look directly at me. The goon made a grunting sound.

"Mr. Pennyback – funny runnin' into you," he said. "You never did come back to talk about that present for your woman. I'd think a private detective like you would have enough cash to buy that diamond we talked about." The goon started to move in my direction, but Coltrane held up a hand, waving him back against the wall. "Never mind 'bout that, though. You mind tellin' me how my business here is any concern of yours?"

There was no steam in his voice, and his eyes swung back and forth, looking from Nkrumah to me. I looked at Nkrumah and smiled.

"I've been hired by Mr. Nkrumah to deal with what he views as a community health problem. You might say I'm a pest exterminator."

It took a few seconds for that to penetrate his brain. Not so his goon, who growled deep in his throat and shifted against the wall. Coltrane frowned.

"Now, ain't no call you be dissin' me like

that. I just here to help these people make more money, that's all."

"Did you ever think maybe they prefer to make their money honestly?"

"I'm a legitimate business man," he said, thumping his chest. "I sell quality merchandise at a good price. I'm just offerin' to let my African brothers and sisters get in on the ground floor and make somethin' better of theyselves."

"What you're *really* trying to do is sink your greedy tentacles into them so you can line your own pockets. If your business was all that legitimate, why is it I can't find any references to it in places where other legitimate businesses are listed? I can't because you're running a scam operation which you prefer to keep as much under the radar as possible. My guess is you want to expand into this community to further mask your con games. Well, the people here are not having any of your con, so you might as well leave."

He blinked at me. His mouth dropped open. The goon shoved off the wall.

"Boss, you want me to take this fucker outside and learn him some manners?" he asked, clearly hoping the answer would be yes.

I remained seated.

Coltrane blinked some more. He shook his head as if to clear his ears, and then frowned down at me.

"Yeah, kid," he said. "You take him outside and show him that it ain't nice to be disrespectin' us honest businessmen. Pennyback, I do hope you got good medical insurance, 'cause you gone need it."

I almost laughed at the way he kept calling someone twice his size 'kid.' But I restrained myself, and continued to sit quietly as the 'kid' started moving away from the wall, with a wide smile on his ugly face.

I watched them both – Coltrane's wolfish smile, and the look of anticipatory glee on the goon's face as he took his time approaching me. I waited until he was about three feet away, and planting his feet shoulder width apart as he leaned forward, both hands outstretched to grab my shoulders.

The dolt never saw it coming.

With a quick snap, I drove my right foot up into his crotch. He made a sound like 'unh, eep,' with his lips pursed and his eyes clenched shut. His forward motion stopped as he bent forward at the waist, and his grasping hands went for his crotch. At the same time, I whipped my right fist up and smashed it into his nose and upper lip. I felt his front teeth cave in as a gush of bright red blood flew around my fist from his nose. His head flew backwards and his mouth opened in a big 'O,' giving me a look at the empty space where his upper teeth once were. Blood poured from his mouth. One hand moved from his crotch to his nose and mouth, and he made mumbling sounds as he felt his misshapen nose. Tears squeezed from his closed eyes, flowing over his stubbled cheeks and mingling with the blood from his nose and mouth.

Coltrane's smile turned into a look of shock, and his face went pale as he looked from me to the ruined face of his henchman. He grasped the edge of the desk, leaning against it, breathing heavily.

"Mudda fuggah, you broge by dose," the goon said when he could finally speak. Little droplets of blood flew from his mouth as he mumbled. "He broge by dose."

Coltrane was now looking ashen as he swayed, averting his eyes from the bloody mess in front of him. He made little 'uh' sounds, and looked as if he was about to vomit.

His goon, still in pain, but recovering a bit, glared murderously at me. "I gode gill you, muddah fuggah." He stumbled toward me, but was distracted by the sound of Coltrane gurgling.

His desire for revenge warred with his obligation to his boss, who looked as if he would faint. Coltrane made a few more murmuring sounds, and then weakly reached for him. "G-get me out of here, Billy," he said in a choked voice, still not looking at the man's bloody face. "Now!"

Billy hesitated. Then, keeping his face averted, he took his boss by the shoulder and the two of them stumbled to the door. I followed them, and when they were outside on the landing, closed the door firmly and turned to Nkrumah. His expression was enigmatic.

Finally, he smiled. "I suppose that was unavoidable," he said. "Actually, it was less violent than it could have been. I applaud your restraint."

"Let's hope it was enough to cause them to reevaluate their plans," I said.

Charles Ray

Death and Taxis

Sixteen

I was back in my office by ten. My description of the encounter with Coltrane and company gave Heather a chuckle, followed immediately by a frown.

"Aren't you a bit worried they might decide to try and get revenge?" she asked. "I mean, you sound like you really embarrassed them."

"I doubt it," I said. "You should have seen Coltrane. When he saw the blood on his thug's face, I thought he'd pass out. No, I think the fight's gone out of that bunch."

Now, we could concentrate on who was killing DC's cab drivers. That little puzzle kept eluding me, though. Buster hadn't been able to pick up anything indicating that any of the gangs were getting together, and Heather was still waiting for the cab companies to get her their call logs. I was at loose ends.

So, I did what I usually do when I'm at that point in a case when I can't decide what to do. I sat in my office alternately staring out the window at the leafless trees, staring at the blank computer screen, and staring at the almost equally blank walls.

Usually this blank period hits me at about the mid-point of an investigation when I've piled up more leads than I can deal with, and have multiple motives and suspects to sort out. I need the quiet time to see the grains of wheat nestled in the chaff. In this case, I was staring at nothingness. I had victims, and Buster's idea of motive – which still didn't make a lot of sense – but, no suspects. For someone who likes puzzles, this was the perfect case. It was like one of those crosswords that have no black squares and no numbers, so you not only have to guess the answers, but you have to figure out where in the damn grid to put them. It was the perfect puzzle, but like the perfect puzzle, it was also frustrating. You see, what I actually like to do is *solve* puzzles. I like them when they're challenging – not when they're impossible. At this point, you're probably beginning to get the picture. This one was drifting closer and closer to the impossible category. And, I wasn't even getting paid for it.

I wasn't in a mood to deal with bureaucrats. When the call button on my phone lit up at the same time my door pushed open, and I heard Heather say, "You can't just barge in like that." I looked up to see one of the bureaucrats I was particularly not in a mood to deal with.

Police Captain Robert Helsing stood in my door trying to freeze me with his frosty glance. Heather stood behind him, the phone in her hand, and an angry look on her face.

"Sorry, boss," she said over his shoulder. "He wouldn't wait for me to call you."

"Do you usually just barge into people's offices without an invitation, captain?" I asked in my best 'offended bureaucrat' tone.

"Listen, Pennyback. I don't have time to play games with you," he said in his "I'm a bureaucrat of higher rank' tone. "I need to talk to you, so tell your girl here to chill her jets."

I imagine Heather wanted to hit him as much as I did. He wasn't just an idiot, he was a chauvinistic idiot.

"In the first place," I said. "Ms. Bunche is not my *girl*, she's my partner, and in the second place, I'm not sure I want to talk to *you*, so why don't you turn your ass around and get the hell out of our office."

I came around the desk and walked over until my face was only inches from his. His breath was stale, and his face smelled of some fruity aftershave. He backed away.

"I advise you against getting physical, Pennyback. The penalty for assaulting a police officer is pretty stiff."

"I reckon I might be getting out of jail about the same time you'd be coming out of intensive care. Of course, there are two of us and only one of you. I imagine we could come up with a pretty good case for police brutality. It might not stick, but the smell would cling for a long time."

His face paled. I think he worried more about the possibility of negative PR than getting his ass stomped. "Okay, okay," he said, holding his hands up, palms out. "Maybe I came on a bit strong. Sorry." He turned to Heather. "My apologies, Ms. Bunche – no offense was intended." Back to me. "Now, could I please talk to you for a few minutes?"

Leopards can't change their stripes, and bureaucrats can't suddenly grow souls. I wasn't fooled at all by his sudden change in manner. But, if he wanted something badly enough to try and play nice, I'd give him a shot.

"Okay, a few minutes. Come in and sit

down."

I went back behind my desk and slouched in the chair. No sense letting him think I was interested in what he had to say. He sat on my uncomfortable visitor's chair. Hopefully it would encourage him to make his visit short.

"Look," he said after sitting. "There's no sense beating around the bush. You and your partner are helping Lieutenant Mayweather, and you're going at cross purposes to my investigation. I know he's a friend of yours, but he's barking up the wrong tree on this one, and if you don't want to see him get in trouble, you'll talk him off it."

"Why are you so sure he's wrong?" I asked.

"Just because two, no three, of the victims happened to be his CIs doesn't mean the case is related to what he's working on. It's just an uptick in street crime, and my task force is all over it. His investigation and your meddling are just getting in the way."

"So, just common street crime? No other criminal activity involved in this?"

"Well, of course, the victims were robbed after they were killed," he said. "But, that's consistent with some robberies. We're just dealing with a particularly vicious perp or perps in these cases."

"Buster – Lieutenant Mayweather – thinks the other killings were just a cover for taking out his informants, and that this is a gang trying to move in on a certain territory in the city. Why do you discount that theory?"

"The lieutenant's been working gang activity too long. He sees a gang hand behind everything that happens. In my task force, we see the reports from all over the department, and there are no indications of any special gang activity to support it, ergo, it's just street crime, and it's not his jurisdiction. I've been lenient so far and not reported his interference. If you can't get him to back off, I'll be forced to take it up the chain of command."

I looked at him through the narrowed slits my lids had made. The idiot was actually trying to threaten me – well, to threaten Buster, but through me. The urge to smack him up side his head came back. I put my hands under my thighs and took a deep breath.

"If you know Buster, you must know that you don't get him to back off a case if he thinks he's right. And, for the record, I think he's right in this case, and it's you who is barking up the wrong tree."

He looked offended, as if no one had ever accused him of being wrong before.

"All of the evidence points to ordinary street crime," he said. "What do either of you have to make me think differently?

I hesitated a bit too long before responding.

"That's what I thought," he continued. "You got *nothing*. Now, I'm asking you again – nicely – get your buddy to back off."

Then, I remembered one little item that did point to something other than normal street crime. "I'll think about it," I said. "If you can explain to me why the feds are also interested in your case."

His mouth dropped open. His face contorted in an expression between puzzled and constipated. "W-what feds?" he asked.

Well, how about that. He didn't know about the smuggling investigation. Score one for Heather's snooping skills. I just *had* to stick it in deeper and twist it a little.

"The feds who are investigating at least one of the dead cab drivers for international smuggling – diamonds I believe. Are you telling me they're investigating on your turf and they haven't told you about it?"

Have you ever seen a fish after you've pulled it from the water and dropped it in the bottom of the boat? It sort of lies there flapping its tail, looking all glassy eyed as its mouth opens and closes. That's what Helsing looked like. The color of his face was even very close to the color of a fish's belly – all pale and icky. It took him several gulps before he found his voice.

"W-where did you g-get this information?"

"Sorry, but I'm not at liberty to divulge the source of my information," I said. "But, until you can explain to me how an international smuggling ring operating right under your nose is normal street crime, I believe I'll continue to help Buster."

"Now, look here, Pennyback," he sputtered. "I can run you in for obstructing my investigation, so you'd be wise to cooperate."

If that was the best he could do he was terribly outclassed. I could see why Buster felt the way he did about him. He was definitely minor league.

"If I was withholding information that was material to your investigation, you might have a case," I said. "But if the federal authorities haven't seen fit to fill you in on what they're doing, it's not my job to do it – hell; I've probably run afoul of them by even telling you. As to *where* I got the information about what they're doing – that's hardly material."

He got a look on his face like a puppy that's been hit across the nose with a newspaper for peeing on the carpet. He was whipped, and he knew it. It was clear, though, that he didn't like it.

"You haven't heard the last of me," he said. He puffed out his chest and wagged a finger at me. "I'll be watching you like a hawk. You put one foot out of line and I'll have your ticket pulled so fast it'll make your head spin."

Like hell, I thought. I just smiled up at him. His face turned red. I was enjoying this much more than I should have been. What I needed to be doing, instead of sitting here jawing with an idiot, was hitting the streets to find the cabbie killers.

"You do what you have to do, captain." I decided to throw him a bone. "If I learn anything that relates to your street crime investigation, I'll be sure to pass it along. In the meantime, I think I'll just keep poking around to see if maybe there's something else going on. Now, if there's nothing else, I have important *investigating* to do."

He wasn't too smart, but he wasn't a total idiot. He knew when he was being told to buzz off. He made a growling sound deep in his throat, and abruptly stood. He opened his mouth as if to say something, and then closed it, glaring down at me. I looked at him with a bland expression that said, 'give it your best shot, bub.' I could almost hear the wheels whirring in his head as he tried to think of something cutting to say, decided against it, and spun on his heels and marched out without even saying goodbye.

Seventeen

I heard the outer door slam, and a few seconds later Heather came into my office carrying her steno pad.

"What a pill," she said. "I could hear him outside in my office. The nerve of him, threatening to arrest you – he can't do that, can he?"

"He could try, but, he'd regret it. Look, forget about him. What have you found out about our cab drivers?"

She flipped the pad open. "Well, I went back to my contact over at Justice. Turns out that two of the other drivers – not Buster's people – were also suspected of being in league with the same smugglers as Nkomo."

"I don't get it," I said. "How do cab drivers help smugglers? Drug pushers I could understand, but diamonds? It makes no sense."

She flipped another page of the pad. "It didn't make sense to me at first. But, according to Bernadette – that's my friend at Justice, we went to secretarial school together – said they were being used as couriers. Seems that the smugglers send packages on flights from overseas through airports in Newark and Atlanta to National. They think the smugglers do it that way because it's cheaper than paying the cost of an airline ticket for a mule. According to her, they think the shipping documents are mailed to the drivers, and they meet the flights and receive the packages and then deliver them to someone here in the DC area. The problem is that the shipments are irregular and there were random pickups, so they've never been able to catch one of them in the act."

I'm no expert on smuggling, but it made sense. There are usually so many cab drivers outside the airport, especially when lots of flights are coming in, it would be hard to notice one going in and picking up a package. If he was parked at the end of the cab queue, he could go in, get the goods, and get back in his car to wait for a legitimate passenger. With thousands of cabs on Washington's streets, from hundreds of companies, trying to track down a specific car and driver would be difficult.

Someone, though, had figured it out. Maybe, I thought, it was someone trying to move in on the smugglers, by robbing their couriers. Whoever it was, was doing it by going after cabs at random, and got lucky with three of them. On the other hand, it could, like Helsing thought, have been a robbery that netted a package of diamonds, and now whoever did the first one was going after cab drivers on the off chance that they'd get another – and they'd been successful with two. If my second scenario was the way it was going down, it could get pretty bloody, and being a Washington cab driver could become a very dangerous line of work.

Heather paled when I shared that theory with her. "What about the trip sheets? Have any of the companies come through yet?"

Flip, flip – more pages of her steno pad fluttered. "I got answers back from five of the companies, including the two that Buster's first two dead informants worked for. In all five cases, the last trip was a call for pickup in Southeast, within a block of Washington Navy Yard. With all the civilian workers there, no one thinks twice about it. In each case, the destination was within a few miles of where the bodies were found. Oh, and, the last place they were before that call was National Airport."

"Any ID on the passengers?" I asked. "National Airport you say?"

She shook her head. "No, the trip sheets only show pickup address and time, number of passengers – one in each case – and destination. Yes, the drivers who the feds suspect of involvement with the smugglers each made a drop off at National before picking up the fare near the Navy Yard."

"Do they show the phone number from which the call was made?"

"The drivers have it," she said. "It's not on the trip sheet. I called a friend in metro police, who told me they didn't find that information on any of the dead drivers. Whoever killed them must have taken it."

Again, it made sense. The killer wouldn't want to leave any traces. There was only one thing I could think of to do.

"I guess I'll have to pound a little pavement," I said. "Give me what you have. I'm going over to the Navy Yard area to ask around. Maybe a merchant or street person saw something that might help."

"Wouldn't the police have already done that?"

"Yeah, even a dope like Helsing would think of that. But, I doubt if he'd be willing to share his information with us."

Charles Ray

Eighteen

The Washington Navy Yard area is only one subway stop from the area where our office is, but it might as well be on another planet. Once you go east on M Street past the Waterfront Metro Station, the environment changes from somewhat seedy, but undergoing gentrification, to blackboard jungle on steroids. The buildings are stained so much by pollution it's almost impossible to tell the original color of the siding; sidewalks are an obstacle course of litter, ranging from empty booze bottles to used condoms; and, questionable looking characters lounge against building walls in every block. Not a place I'm comfortable parking a car – even my Volkswagen – so, I walked to the metro, bought a ticket, and rode the green line the one stop to the Naval Yard station.

It was the middle of the day, so the train wasn't crowded. Just a few navy guys in uniform, probably on their way from the Pentagon to the Navy Yard, some rough looking characters in stained jeans with hard hats clipped to their belts, a couple of street toughs with baggy pants hanging low on their hips exposing their underwear, and a harried looking old lady who clutched her Bible to her chest and kept her eyes on the floor of the car.

I came out of the station a block west of the main gate to the Navy Yard, and headed north toward L Street; one of the pickup addresses on the list Heather had given me. It was the pickup point for Dudu Nkomo the morning he was killed.

The address was at the corner of L and New Jersey Avenue, close enough to the Navy Yard not to arouse any suspicion. As I neared the spot, in fact, I noticed at least two men dressed in the standard bureaucrat's uniform – off the rack blue suit and wingtip shoes – coming out of a newsstand near the corner. Probably a lot of the civilians who worked for the navy took cabs to get around town rather than the subway. Even in the crisp autumn air there was the smell of unwashed bodies, stale booze, urine, and desperation. I entered the newsstand which was being run by a skinny, swarthy man with a hooked nose and crooked teeth, who eyed me with a mixture of hope and suspicion. The temperature inside the shop was twenty degrees higher than outside, and the odor was dusty with an overlay of the flowery smell of curry.

When I approached the counter behind which he stood rather than going to the racks of magazines and newspapers, his look of suspicion deepened. I noticed that his right hand slid under the counter – to reach a panic button or gun, I wasn't sure, and decided not to take chances. Slowly, I removed my PI license from my pocket and held it up so he could see it. "I'd like to ask you a few questions, if you don't mind," I said.

An expression of boredom replaced the suspicion.

"I see very little," he said in the clipped off, hard to understand speech of South Asia. He was either Indian or Pakistani, and my money was on the latter, because Indians are so status conscious it was unlikely one of them would run a newsstand in a depressed black area of town. "Customers come and go – I do not remember most of them unless they cause trouble."

"It's not about customers," I said. "I imagine a lot of people hail cabs just outside your shop."

"I suppose they do. Many workers from

the Navy Yard buy newspapers from me. But, I have enough to worry about inside here with the kids who come and try to shoplift candy or magazines. If you wish to know what goes on outside, you should ask some of the vagrants who hang about."

So much for shopkeepers who know the neighborhood, I thought. I thanked him for his time and went back outside. The smell of curry still lingered in my nostrils, now mixing with the stench of the exterior. I looked around, and off to the left, huddling over a grate from which white puffs emanated, I saw a wreck of a human being, draped in a dirty olive drab field jacket with a knit cap pulled down over his ears. As I approached, he regarded me warily through bloodshot eyes. Next to him on the sidewalk was a dented coffee can with a crudely lettered cardboard sign which read, 'Help the Homeless.'

When I stopped in front of him, he looked up at me and smiled, showing gaps in his mouth. "Hey, bro, you got some spare change for a homeless veteran?" He held up a hand in a tattered black glove with half the fingers missing. His dark brown fingers were ashy from the cold and his fingernails were uneven and dirt encrusted. He didn't have the look of an ex-military man, but I didn't have all that much experience with the homeless, and if he'd been on the streets long, he could have changed.

I pulled my wallet out and extracted a twenty. He licked his chapped lips and his smile broadened as he reached for it.

I pulled the bill back. "You'll have to work for this, friend."

He frowned. "What you want me to do? I can't do no heavy liftin' on account I got a bad back and arthritis."

"No heavy lifting," I said. "I just need a bit of information."

He licked his lips again. "What you wanta know, man?"

"Have you been here long?"

"Long enough. This all the home I got since I done got kicked outa the shelter over in Anacostia."

I didn't want to know why he'd been kicked out to the street – I didn't need to know – it was apparent from the smell of stale booze that hit me in the face every time he opened his mouth.

"I need to know if you've seen anyone recently get into a cab around here."

"I see lots of folk get in taxis. When you talkin' 'bout in particular?"

"This would have been either early Tuesday morning," I said.

He closed his eyes and cocked his head to one side, scratching at the wool cap. "Yeah, now you mention it, I did see a dude get in a taxi Tuesday mornin'. It was early, just fo breakfast. I figure he's one of them brothers what work the night shift at the navy yard, you know."

"He was a black man? What did he look like?"

"I wasn't payin' much 'tention, know what I mean. He just a black dude. Big muthah, wearin' a brown overcoat. He was totin' a briefcase just like lots of them folk over the navy yard have. Oh yeah, and he was wearin' gloves."

"Nothing unusual about that in this weather." Said the man who'd forgotten his own gloves at home on this chilly morning.

"Naw, 'cept he didn't have no cold weather gloves. He was wearin' them gloves like they wear over to the hospital."

That got my attention. Who wears surgical gloves outside, and in the cold at that? I pressed him for a more detailed description, and as sketchy as it was, it sounded a lot like Coltrane's goon.

The case was getting stranger by the minute.

Nineteen

I joined the home-bound commuters from the Navy Yard on the subway, thankfully only for one stop. The car was jammed with tired, haggard looking man and women who had just spent a day in a boring office, on their way home to their boring homes in the suburbs. Even the normally loud teenagers were subdued. I wasn't able to get a seat - instead, I was sandwiched between a fat woman and a beefy construction worker near the door.

The little shopping center near Waterfront Metro station was crowded with last minute shoppers, as were the sidewalks all the way to my office. In addition, the temperature had dropped several degrees, and I'd forgotten to wear gloves that morning. My fingers were numb by the time I got to the office.

As soon as I entered the warmer office, my

fingers started tingling, then aching. I blew on them trying to get some circulation going.

Heather looked up from her computer. "Cold outside?" she asked. I glared back at her.

"I'll be in my office until my hands are warm," I said. "Then, we're closing up and going home."

"Would you like a cup of warm tea?" she asked my departing back.

My first inclination was to snort and say no, but then, a warm cup would be just the thing to wrap my fingers around. "Sounds great," I said.

I was still wearing my jacket and huddled in my chair when she brought the tea in. She'd put it in the big mug I occasionally use for coffee. When I took it from her, the warmth of the ceramic felt good – really good. I blew on it and thanked her.

The tea smelled like a flower shop, and I could only guess what it tasted like. It didn't matter, though, because I had no intention of drinking it. I was enjoying the soothing massage of the heat waves from the cup on my shriveled fingertips which were beginning to get some feeling back at last. I just sat there with my hands wrapped tightly around that cup, wishing the heat to last.

The red light on my phone set came on and blinked. I looked at my watch. It was half past four. Unless it was a matter of life or death, it would wait for tomorrow, I thought. All I wanted was to get home and cuddle my cold body against Sandra's warmth. I pushed the answer button. "Yeah, Heather, what is it?"

"You have visitors," she said.

"Is it important?"

"They say it is."

Of course they would, but Heather's a good judge of character, and there was nothing in her tone to indicate she didn't believe them. I looked at my watch again. I could spare half an hour.

"Okay, send them in."

They looked important. At first glance, they looked wealthy. You had to look a second time to see the hard edges. A third glance would show you the bulges beneath their coats. Didn't mean they weren't important. Did mean they were possibly dangerous.

They were about the same height – five eleven or so – and about the same build – around one-sixty – but, there the resemblance ended. One was broad shouldered with close-cropped blond hair and mean blue eyes, while the other was slender and a bit stooped, with lank brown hair and watery brown eyes. The blond wore a gray pin striped suit under a tan overcoat, while his companion wore a dark blue three piece without overcoat. They smelled of expensive cologne.

"Come in, gentlemen," I said. "Sorry I don't have seats for both of you, but I don't normally get so many visitors."

"That is of no importance," the blond one said. "We will not take much of your time. We have need of your services."

I couldn't quite place his accent. It sounded faintly Eastern European, but there was something in the cadence that was off.

He walked around to the left side of my desk, while his partner moved to the right. Their suits looked expensive, but their actions were familiar – they were flanking me. Whatever else they might have been, these two had combat experience.

I was careful to keep my expression bland. Until I knew why they were in my office, they represented a threat, so I decided the best course of action was to play along with them.

"Well, gentlemen, my fee is a thousand a day plus expenses," I said. "And I usually require a week's fee up front. Any funds not used will, of course, be refunded."

They didn't even blink. "That sounds reasonable," the blond said. "But, don't you wish to know what we want you to do?"

"Of course I want to know. I'll tell you now, though, I don't do divorce, I don't do industrial espionage, and I don't collect on gambling debts."

The guy to the right smiled slightly. The blond's face remained as impassive as a granite wall. "I assure you," he said. "We do not require you to do such things. We simply wish you to find certain items that belong to . . . our employer."

"What are these items, and how do you expect me to retrieve them?"

"You do not need to know the exact nature of the items," the guy on the right said with an accent that was even stranger than the blond's. "We will tell you what to look for. As to retrieval – we merely wish you to locate the items. We will take care of retrieving them."

This was getting interesting. While we talked, and despite my impassive expression, my mind was racing. Little pieces of the puzzle were beginning to fall, if not exactly in place, not too far from where they belonged. These two were not American, that much was certain, and they dealt in rough trade, but dressed like Wall Street bankers. High stakes, high risk line of work? Diamond smugglers! Funny how when your mind seems to be running around in circles, it gets you to where you need to go. There were a few pieces of the puzzle that were hovering just out of my line of sight, but I had a feeling that these two would help move me closer to them.

"Okay," I said. "Let's say I take the job. You can't tell me specifically what I'm looking for – what *can* you tell me? And, while you're at it, how about starting with who you are? I like to know the names of my clients."

They looked at each other. The blond nodded. "My name is Henrik van Klerk," the guy on the right said. "My colleague is Moishe Arens. We represent an international conglomerate with offices in several countries, including one right here in Washington."

The names explained the unfamiliar accent. Henrik van Klerk was obviously South African, and the blond was Israeli. Strange bedfellows. But it went a long way toward validating my assumptions about their line of work

"Please to meet you," I said. "Now, what can you tell me about these mysterious items you want me to find?"

"They will be in boxes about the size of a cigar box," Arens said. "Or perhaps even in cloth bags of about the same volume."

"Where were these items last seen?"

More looks passed between them. Arens frowned and shook his head, but van Klerk nodded. "He will need to know that much at least if he is to find the . . . items," he said.

Arens' brows knitted and he blew air through his nose and mouth. I had the feeling he'd ask me to go looking for the 'items' with a blindfold on if he'd had his way. Finally, he shrugged.

"Very well, I suppose you are correct," he said. He turned to face me. "The items, four in all, were picked up at National Airport by individuals who were hired to transport them to their final destination. There were four different deliveries on four different days, and four different couriers. None of the items were delivered to the destination. We suspect the shipments were taken by the same individual or organization. We would like for you to verify that."

It looked like it had pained him to tell me so much, but van Klerk was right – without that information at least, I'd be looking for a specific needle in a haystack full of needles.

"Okay; I'll need the dates of the shipments, and the names of your couriers."

Arens nodded at van Klerk, who reached into his coat and pulled out a single sheet of paper which he handed across the desk to me. On it was the names of four of the murdered cab drivers, one of them was Dudu Nkomo, and the dates of shipments were the same as the dates of the murders. My left eyebrow twitched when I saw Nkomo's name.

"You recognize the names?" Arens asked.

There wasn't much sense in trying to deceive them. I had a gut feeling they knew it anyway. "Yeah," I said. "They came up in the course of another investigation."

"Which," Arens said, smirking. "You're not at liberty to tell us about, of course."

The guy was good, I'd give him that. I admired the skillful way he'd explained why they couldn't tell me any more than they did. The fact that they were involved in illegal activity was, of course, the primary factor, but he'd done a great job of masking that. If Heather hadn't learned of the smuggling investigation, I would, at this point, be taking these two guys for some kind of high level corporate security types. I don't like aiding and abetting a felony, but I had to do a bit of coin flipping. Turn these guys down and maybe miss an opportunity to nab the cabbie killer, or go along with them and work out the moral and ethical details later. I don't like to see people get away with murder, so I mentally held my nose and opted for the latter course of action.

"Good point," I said. "Now, if you'll come with me, I'll have my associate prepare a contract, and you can pay the advance. If you pay by check, I'll have to hold off doing anything until it clears."

"We would . . . rather not have a written contract," van Klerk said, reaching into his jacket and withdrawing a thick black leather wallet. "And, as for your advance, I am assuming that you will also accept cash – will ten thousand be sufficient? And, there will be no need for a refund. Consider this your fee for the job."

Ten grand advance for finding lost items which I already suspected I knew the location of – would it be sufficient? Damn right it would! I get ten grand a month retainer from Holcombe, Stein and Chang, the law firm that my old army buddy Quincy Chang is a partner in. They pay me for doing the occasional odd job. The money is enough to cover Heather's salary plus rent, utilities and other routine expenses. I live on my army retirement pay, and plow the portion of our income that would represent my salary back into the company. An extra ten grand meant that I could buy something nice for Sandra. I took the stack of hundreds he proffered.

"Cash is fine," I said. "And, I guess a handshake and transfer of funds is as good as a written contract. Hell, if you can't trust a man's word, no piece of paper's gonna make him do right."

Their smiles told me this is what they wanted to hear. Arens took a card from his pocket and dropped it on my desk. All it had on it was a local phone number.

"We can be reached at that number at any time," he said. "When you have located the items, please call and tell us where they are. We will take care of it from there."

I suppose I should have been concerned by *how* they would take care of it. I could guess if I really tried. I should also probably have been curious about why they'd come to me instead of some other agency, or even some of the local gangs. But, I decided not to go down that road just in case it caused me to reevaluate my decision to work with these guys.

We shook hands, and they left as quietly as they'd come.

I sat there for a long time after they'd gone, wondering whether or not I'd just made a deal with the devil.

Twenty

After turning the cash over to Heather to be deposited in our bank account, I hopped in the Bug and headed home. I explained that the clients preferred paying cash and didn't need a contract, but left out the details of the discussion. I felt a little guilty about that, but the less she knew the less chance she'd be in any trouble if things went sour.

Traffic crossing the District was maddening, and it got worse on River Road from the Beltway all the way to the turnoff to my farm. It was after six when I finally reached the warmth of my living room.

Sandra was sitting on the couch listening to classical music on the one radio station we both listen to frequently, wrapped in a blanket despite the coziness of the room, sipping cocoa from a large mug.

I offered to cook supper – to which she readily agreed, promising to join me in the kitchen as soon as the stove had brought the ambient temperature up to egg hatching level. I had shucked my jacket and was on my way to the kitchen when the phone rang. It was Carlton Raine, inviting the two of us to join him and Elizabeth Sung for dinner. Sandra frowned at the prospect of going out into the cold, even if it was only a few steps to the car, and it would still be warm, but brightened up when I reminded her that Blood's living room was always kept warm, and it meant the two of us wouldn't have to do any clean up after eating.

She went to the bedroom to get a heavy coat, and I climbed back into my jacket. She huddled against me when we went outside, and only let go when I'd helped her into the passenger side. She sat hugging herself until the Volkswagen's heater brought the interior temperature up high enough to make me feel a little uncomfortable in my jacket.

By the time we got to Blood's place, my armpits were sticky with sweat, but she was smiling contentedly.

Blood, who hated cold weather as much as Sandra did, wasn't waiting on his front porch as usual, but the door was ajar. His signal for us to come on in and letting us know he knew we were there. The transition from the car to the outside air was rough – the cold hit my overly warmed body like a paddle with tacks in it. We both dashed for the door, and only my innate sense of chivalry made me let her enter first.

"Welcome kids," Blood said. "Close that door. You're letting all the warm air out."

He crossed the room and kissed Sandra's cheeks, and then turned and shook my hand. His hand was warm and dry. Elizabeth Sung, her ample figure well displayed in a furry brown jump suit, came in from the kitchen carrying a tray with a coffee urn and four cups on it. She placed the tray on the big coffee table in front of the sofa and hugged Sandra, doing the air kiss routine to keep from smudging makeup – hers most likely – and then presented her porcelain smooth cheek for me to lightly kiss. I gave her a semi-air kiss, just grazing her smooth, warm flesh. She smelled of jasmine.

"Take those coats off and grab seats," she said. "You two look like you could use a hot cup of coffee."

Sandra grabbed a cup, holding it against her breasts, as soon as Elizabeth poured it. I was a little more controlled. I waited for her to hand it to me before cupping it in my hands, letting the warmth penetrate. I noticed something familiar about the aroma.

"Is there chicory in this coffee?" I asked.

"Yes, Carlton insists on it. He says it's the way his grandmother made it. I have to admit, it does add to the flavor."

That it does. It was the way I remember the old folks making coffee when I was a kid; they said to take the bitterness out.

Blood walked over and put a hand around Elizabeth's waist. "Hon, why don't you go put the finishing touches on supper," he said. "I have something I need to discuss with Al here."

She gave him a strange look. Then she smiled that hundred watt smile of hers. "Sure. Let me know when you two have finished your little boy talk. Sandra, would you like to help me in the kitchen?"

"Is it as warm there as here?" Sandra asked, looking up from her coffee.

"Warmer," Elizabeth said. "And, Carlton is baking his special honey ham, so the aroma is absolutely delicious."

The two women, with arms linked, walked past us, and a fine looking sight the two of them made walking away. Elizabeth was a bit slimmer in the hips than Sandra, but only by a little, and what she lacked in bulk, she made up for in movement. Out of the corner of my eye, I noticed that Blood was enjoying the view as much as I was.

He recovered before I did. "Pull your eyes back in your head, son," he said. "And, come with me. I've something you need to hear."

Inside his control room, with the door securely shut, he had me sit at the monitor console.

"Why do you close the door?" I asked. "There's no one else here but Elizabeth and Sandra."

"Need to know, son. What Elizabeth doesn't know about what I do can't hurt her. Now, listen carefully. I'm going to play you a tape that I think you might find very interesting."

He tapped a few keys and the familiar hiss of static came from the speakers, followed immediately by the sound of footsteps on gravel.

"You ogay, bod?" I recognized the sound of Wilson, Coltrane's goon, and from the slurred speech, this must have been right after our encounter in Joseph Nkrumah's office.

"No, I ain't okay, Billy." Coltrane's voice. Next, there was the sound of retching. *"Get some of them wipes outa the trunk and get that blood off your face."*

More crunching of footsteps. More retching. Then a creaking sound and the crackling of cloth or paper, followed by a metallic thump. A long moment of silence.

"Okay, boss, I done wiped it all off. I can breathe better now, too. You want something to wipe your face?"

"I want you to get me the hell back to my office. I need a drink to settle my stomach."

The sound of a door slamming and a hum as the Cadillac's engine was fired up. Then silence.

"The mike shuts off when talking stops, or when it detects a steady droning noise like an engine," Blood said. "If they start to talk, it'll immediately come on again."

Coltrane must not have felt like talking, because all I heard was the slight hissing. Blood tapped another key.

The sound of the car door opening and closing, and footsteps on a hard surface fading away, and then more silence.

Another key tap, and there was the sound of a door closing. A short time later there was a soft hissing sound that I couldn't identify.

Then, Coltrane's voice came clearly from the speaker. *"You want a shot, Billy? Not that* you deserve it, letting Pennyback get the best of you like that."

"Aw, come on, boss. Ain't my fault. I didn't know that niggah was gone kick me in the nuts like that. Shit, that hurt. Then, he done gone and broke my nose."

"You might oughta get that nose looked at."

"It don't hurt much now."

"Yeah, but you gone have another bump in it. You oughta get a doctor to fix it up."

"Hell, I don't mind the bumps. Bitches might like it. It make me look dangerous. 'Sides, only thing gone make me feel better is to shove a blade in that niggah's gut."

"We ain't got time for that shit, Billy. We got to stick to the plan. You done throwed us off bad 'nuff with your freelancin'."

"Aw, I couldn't just leave somethin' like that layin' 'round, boss. That was like found money, you dig. Who would of thought them damn cab drivers would be drivin' round with shit like that in they cars?"

"I ain't blamin' you – just sayin' it's done throwed our schedule off. We got to get back on track."

"What you gone do with the stuff, boss?"

"Got me a contact up in New York gone

come down and look it over next week. He done already told me he pay me five hundred grand for the lot. I know the sumbitch cheatin' me, but don't matter. I didn't pay for 'em, so it all be profit, you hear what I'm sayin'? And your cut of it be fifty big ones."

"Now, that's what I'm talkin' 'bout. And, when we finish takin' over and all, can I go kill that sumbitch, Pennyback?"

"Shit, I reckon you done earned that, Billy boy. Be my guest."

Blood tapped a key and the sound stopped.

"Any of that make sense to you, son? I mean, other than one mad son of a bitch who wants to cut out your liver for breaking his nose, none of it makes sense to me. I thought this guy Coltrane was out of the picture. I mean, I just left the recorder going because you hadn't told me it was done – and, a good thing I did it appears."

"So did I – but, apparently I was wrong," I said. "In fact, it sounds like he just might be the main act in this little drama."

"I know it's not necessary, but you will be careful about this guy, won't you?"

"I'm not too worried about him," I said. "He doesn't strike me as the subtle type. If he comes at me, he'll either come at me straight on, or try to stab me in the back. Either way, I think I can handle it."

I hoped I was right. But, if my interpretation of what I'd just heard was correct, there was a lot more to Coltrane than I'd first thought. It would depend on how much he was controlling his hired gun – or knife. I felt a bit foolish thinking about it. I'd completely ignored the possibility that Coltrane was behind the extortion through murder. My mistake had been judging him by his appearance. He dressed like a pimp, and strutted around like the king of the walk, and that had distracted me. I'd seen him for trying to horn in on the legitimate business of the community, but not working such an elaborate scheme as using terror to get his way.

I was guessing, but I'm pretty good at guessing, and I'm usually right. The operation he was referring to could very well be as low level as I'd first thought. What I was fairly sure of was the reference to the items his goon had delivered to him. That had to be the diamonds the drivers were carrying for my two visitors. If he had the diamonds, that meant he'd been involved in the murders, and that meant he *had* to be behind the effort to establish a gang presence in the community.

My expression must have shown what I

was thinking. Blood regarded me with a serious expression.

"There's something you're not telling me, son," he said simply.

And, indeed there was. It had been lurking in the back of my mind ever since I shook hands with the two strangers in my office. Oh sure, I could argue that they'd never come right out and said they were international smugglers, but that would be splitting hairs. I *knew* what they were, and in a sense, by accepting their money, I was now aiding and abetting their crime. At the time I decided to go along with them, it hadn't been clear to me why I should do it, but I think my subconscious was at work. I was looking for a weapon to use against Deacon Coltrane, even though I didn't really know that at the time. Now, though, the recording cinched it. It dropped enough of the final pieces in place that the final picture, while not complete, was recognizable. The problem was, I didn't have enough hard evidence to take it to Buster – I couldn't tell him about the bugs and GPS tracker, as they weren't exactly being legally used. That room in the back of my mind where the *real* thinking takes place had probably known all along that Coltrane was behind everything. I'd just let the 'take the easy way' part of my brain discount him because of surface appearances.

What I was thinking of doing wasn't quite legal either, and it troubled me. While there was no doubt that Coltrane was a bad man, up to no good, under the law he was still entitled to due process. Buster would, I know, see that he got every right that he was entitled to even though he might want to vomit while doing it. The question was: did I have the same obligation? Or, did ridding the community of vermin like Coltrane justify any means used in doing so?

A burden shared, they say, is a burden lightened. I couldn't share it with Buster, Sandra, or Heather, and my buddy Quincy is an officer of the court – so, of course, I could never breathe a word of it to him. Carlton Raine, on the other hand, had spent his entire adult life working in the shadow world of intelligence, and had, no doubt, done things that he'd never tell his mother about. He might understand.

I dumped it all on him – my suspicions about Coltrane, the two mysterious figures who came to my office, and my idea of how to use them to get Coltrane to lay off Nkrumah's community. When I'd finished, he sat silently regarding me for several seconds.

When he finally spoke, his voice was soft, but firm. "Al, I know how you feel right now. When I first started working for the agency, I felt that way – a lot. You're raised to obey the law and try to do right, and then you find yourself in a situation where, in order to do the right thing by the ones you're sworn to protect, you have to do something that seems awfully wrong – that, according to our laws, *is* wrong."

"How do you deal with it?"

"Different people deal with it in different ways," he said. "Some of the guys I know took to drink. A few wound up having to be put in long-term therapy – I think one guy even ended up being institutionalized. The majority, though, just told themselves that it was for the greater good, and if they didn't do it, someone else would. Life's like that, son. Sometimes you have to choose between options – both bad – and go for the one that does the least harm – or that does good for your side, which you hope is the good guys."

"The immigrants in Nkrumah's community are the innocents here. If I do nothing, Coltrane will sink his hooks into the neighborhood and turn it into another cesspool of drugs, hookers, and sidewalks that are dangerous to walk on."

"And, there's nothing the authorities can do to stop him?"

"If I could find some hard evidence linking him to the murders of those cab drivers, they could," I said. "But, all we have are these recordings, which are themselves illegal and cryptic at best. I need a smoking gun to bring this guy down legally."

He rested his chin on his right fist, his eyes half closed. Then, he made a humming sound in the back of his throat, and looked at me, a wolfish grin splitting his face. "So, maybe what you need is something that will cause Mr. Coltrane to give you that smoking gun."

"I don't think I could appeal to his better nature and just ask him to confess."

"No, but you could appeal to his sense of self preservation, and give him the option of dealing with the authorities who'll read him his Miranda Rights or with a bunch of pissed off smugglers who'll give him a one-way ticket to the bottom of the Anacostia."

"But, what do I do about letting them know where their diamonds are?"

The wolfish grin got wider. "Well, assuming your Mr. Coltrane values his continued existence, you might arrange to have the diamonds in a place for your new clients to retrieve them . . . and, we could arrange a suitable reception for them."

It was bizarre – it was byzantine – but, it could work. It meant double crossing my clients – but, I wouldn't lose a lot of sleep over that – but, it could – no, *would*, I reminded myself, solve two major criminal cases, and close both of mine. The murderer of the cab drivers would be brought to justice, the smugglers would be rolled up, and the threat to the community would be eliminated. The fact that Buster would be able to rub Helsing's face in it when he proved his theory right and Helsing's wrong, was just the dessert at the end of a five-course meal.

"What do you have in mind?" I asked.

He spent the next five minutes, until Elizabeth rapped on the door and called us to dinner, explaining the plan.

Twenty-One

Thursday morning was warm for November. Sandra and I were both sweating by the time we'd finished our run and workout in the barn. After a hot shower together, we fixed a big breakfast, ate, cleaned the kitchen, and left together for work. I followed her until we passed Independence Avenue, where I split off to go to my office, and she turned east toward Carter High School.

Heather's car was in its accustomed space, and our visitor's slot was empty. It was a few minutes after eight, and the parking lot and sidewalks were empty of people. There were only a few other cars in the lot. Most of our fellow tenants were probably hoping the warmer weather would last through the weekend, and were getting an early start.

I pulled the Volkswagen in next to her car and, with my jacket over my arm, headed for the stairway up to our office on the second level.

When I reached the top of the stairs, I noticed a strange odor first – a smell of stale booze and sweat, and then I caught sight of movement on my right out of the corner of my eye.

Wilson, Coltrane's number one goon, rose from behind a large packing crate. His eyes were bloodshot, and he needed a shave. From the odor wafting from his body as the air blew my way, he also needed a shower. He had a dirty dressing across the bridge of his nose, and I noticed that he made a slight whistling sound when he breathed. He had his hands in the pockets of the tan overcoat he wore.

I turned to face him. "What are you doing here?" I asked.

He didn't seem to focus directly on me – rather, a point a few feet behind me. "Boss said wait," he mumbled. "But, I tired of waitin'. You done dissed me in front of people. You can't do that."

He shuffled toward me. I held up a hand.

"It's not a good idea, what you're thinking about," I said. "You're in no condition."

I don't know why I was trying to keep this idiot from getting himself hurt. Maybe the same attitude I have toward cockroaches – they're noxious pests, but I hate stomping on one. If he kept moving toward me, though, I would have no choice but to stomp him.

"I'm gone cut yo heart out, mutha fuckah." Spittle dribbled from the side of his mouth. "You ain't gone be kickin' nobody else in the nuts."

On an intellectual level, I know that time is a constant. But, when you've meditated as long as I have, time also becomes subjective. I've developed the ability, when things get dicey, to mentally slow time so that things around me seem to move in slow motion. I can *feel* movement as well as see it.

His right hand came slowly out of the pocket. There was a 'snick!' sound, and six inches of sharp blade appeared in his hand. He was stoned, or drunk, but it didn't matter, he was dangerous. The fool was going for me in broad daylight right outside my office door practically. Probably thought – if he was still capable of any kind of rational thinking – that he'd be able to get out to the street and away before anyone found the body.

When he was about four feet away, still moving as if he was walking through molasses, he brought the knife up in a thrusting motion and leaned toward me. At that point, time speeded up. I waited until the knife was just inches from my gut before pivoting to the left, letting his hand and the blade slip by almost close enough to slice the fabric of my shirt. With my left hand, I grabbed his wrist, and with my right, pulled my jacket from my left arm and whipped it up and across his face.

The tab on the zipper must have hit his forehead, because a bright crimson line sprang up across it, and blood began seeping down into his brows. I squeezed hard with my left hand, digging the thumb into his wrist. Dropping the jacket, I swung my right fist back around, jamming the middle knuckle into his temple. His mouth gaped open and he made an 'hmph' sound, as his eyes started rolling back in their sockets. I pulled hard with my left hand, swinging around to the left, and sent his body sailing over the wooden railing. I heard a thump as his body hit the gravel parking lot. Looking down, I saw that, luckily, he'd landed in our visitor parking slot. He was lying flat on his back with his arms outstretched as if on a crucifix.

I picked up my jacket and rushed down the stairs. Kneeling, I felt a pulse in his neck. Then, I pulled out my phone and dialed 911.

Twenty-Two

A police squad car and an ambulance from DC Fire Department arrived at about the same time – in record time for the neighborhood in fact. A slightly overweight uniformed officer took my initial statement as the EMTs were loading Wilson onto a gurney and putting him in the ambulance. The cop's partner retrieved the knife from the balcony, and went in the ambulance with him after handcuffing him to the rail of the gurney.

I was sketchy about what happened, telling the cop that I thought he might just be a drunk who saw me as a potential mugging victim. The smell of booze on his breath supported that, but the expensive overcoat he was wearing caused the cop to look at me strangely.

"Maybe he stole the coat," I said helpfully.

That seemed to placate him. And, after Heather came out of the office he stopped paying much attention to me completely, taking my name and phone number and asking me to remember to come to the precinct to file charges.

The driver's license in his wallet had identified Coltrane's goon as William Henry Wilson, and gave a residence address in Anacostia not far from Coltrane's office. Wilson looked a lot older than the twenty-eight indicated by his license. He'd be a bit older when he got out of jail for assault with a deadly weapon.

His visit had made my mind up, though. I was putting the plan to bring Coltrane down into action without further delay.

Twenty-Three

There were a few things I needed to do, though, before launching my plan.

I spent a few minutes calming Heather down.

"One of these days, you might not be so lucky," she said. "What if that guy had been sober?"

"He would still have been stupid, and that gave me all the advantage I needed," I said. "Look, quit worrying about it. I have another job for you." That perked her up. "I need you to get the name and contact information for the lead federal agent on the smuggling investigation, and I need it yesterday."

She got a curious look on her face, but she was accustomed to my wild requests, so she picked up the phone and dialed.

I could only hear her end of the conversation, but I was impressed with how smoothly she wheedled the necessary information out of whoever it was on the other end of the line. She wrote a name and phone number on a page in her steno pad, hung up, and tore the page out of the pad. She was smiling triumphantly when she handed it to me. There was a local number and the name SAIC Ted Striker. The SAIC stood for Special Agent in Charge – from which of the alphabet soup of federal law enforcement agencies, I didn't know, nor did I particularly care – and the name, 'Striker', had a kind of Captain America ring to it. I could picture this guy: square jaw, brown or sun-bleached hair cropped close to the skull military style, and wearing a dark blue suit that looked like it came off the rack at J.C. Penney – which it probably did.

Despite her look of curiosity, she didn't ask why I wanted the information, and I didn't tell her. Instead, I said, "Thanks. Now, I need you to get on that information about the cab drivers. You know, - schedules, fares, and all that for the day they were killed. I think there might be a pattern there that we're missing."

I didn't think any such thing, but I needed her distracted so I could do what I had to do. She shrugged and turned back to her computer. I went into my office.

I took my jacket off, tossing it on the back of my visitor's chair and sat in my nice leather chair behind my slightly scarred desk and, taking my cell phone out, leaned back and began making a series of calls. I was using my cell rather than the office phone for the same reason I didn't tell Heather why I wanted the federal agent's contact information – I didn't want her even accidentally involved in what I was about to do.

My first call was to Buster. When he came on, I told him about my visit from Coltrane's man, Wilson.

"So, you put that asshole in the hospital?" He laughed. "I hope you broke something."

"I don't know about breaking anything, but I bruised him pretty good. Look, I think you ought to check out the knife he tried to use on me. See if it might be the weapon used on those cab drivers." I gave him the names of the two uniforms who took Wilson into custody. He recognized both.

"You think he's the one who iced my CIs?"

I told him about my conversation with the bum near the Navy Yard. "It adds up," I said. "Coltrane's trying to move in on the community, and he has this thug working for him who likes to use a knife. It's a stretch, but my theory is that Coltrane's using the attempt to buy into the businesses as a distraction from what he's really up to."

"Coltrane and the street gangs? You're right – that is a stretch. But, I'll get to my boys on the beat and the dudes in the lab on the knife. If this Wilson is the killer, that do kind of point the finger back at Coltrane." His ghetto speech was coming back, meaning he was happy.

"In the meantime, I have a few more promising leads I need to track down. If they pan out, we might be able to wrap this thing up soon."

I didn't tell him an outright lie – I just didn't tell him the whole truth. I couldn't tell him what I had planned. As an officer of the law, he had a duty to try and stop me, or violate his oath of office. I wouldn't put him in the position to have to do either.

"Okay, bro," he said. "I let you know if anything come out of this. Glad you didn't get your liver cut out."

I broke the connection and immediately dialed Blood Raine.

"Al," his cultured voice said. "I take it you're ready to put our plan into action?"

"I have a few things to put into place first." I gave him Striker's name and number. "You sure this guy will cooperate?"

"We're giving him a smuggling ring he's been tracking for months," he said. "I'm sure."

"Won't he be curious about how you came by the information?"

He chuckled. "I don't plan on calling him directly. Give me a few minutes to contact the person above him in his chain of command. I'll call you back in a few minutes."

He broke the connection. Blood's like Heather in a way. He has more connections than the phone company from his years with the agency, and I've found it best not to inquire about them. Not that he'd tell me if I asked. Technically, the agency's not allowed to operate on U.S. soil, but they had ways of getting things done, and Blood Raine had years of experience in that shadowy world – experience that made my time in army special operations seem like a Boy Scout Jamboree. If he said he could get it done, it was as good as done.

Ten minutes later my cell phone rang. I recognized Blood's number.

"Yeah," I said. "Is everything set?"

"The pieces are in place and ready to go on your signal. Now, you have to follow my instructions precisely if this is to work. Once you're ready for Striker and his team to move, call me. Give me ten minutes before you make the next call – it'll take that much time for them to get a trace set up." Like Heather's computer skills, I had no real idea how the feds would track the number I'd be calling, but Blood assured me that if I could keep the line open for two minutes, they'd get a fix and have a surveillance team at the location within five minutes. I could picture a bunch of federal agents sitting around in black SUVs with headphones on, just waiting for their instruments to beep or warble, or whatever they did. "After you make the call, it would be wise to get yourself as far away from the scene of action as possible. Oh, and while I'm thinking about it – don't forget to retrieve the tracking devices you put on Coltrane's car and in his office."

Twenty-Four

I told Heather I was running an errand, which strictly speaking was the truth.

The drive from my place to the parking lot adjacent to Coltrane's ratty old building, thanks to traffic, took thirty minutes. Nothing much had changed since my last visit. The same pimple-faced kid was standing near the corner of the building, wearing a Baltimore Ravens jacket this time. When he recognized me, he turned his attention back to the street.

I pulled in next to the purple Cadillac and killed the engine. I sat there for a few moments, making sure no one was paying me any attention. Then I got out and walked to the pimp mobile. Kneeling near the door, I reached under and yanked the listening device off the undercarriage. I then crab-walked toward the rear of the car and reached beneath it, feeling around for the GPS tracker. At first, I missed it. Just as my panic level began to rise my fingers brushed against it. The stronger magnet of the GPS required a stronger force to break its bond with the metal, and it made a scraping sound as I pulled it free.

I slipped both devices into my right jacket pocket, and started around to the front of the building. Pimply-face met me at the corner again.

"Hey," he said. "You back. Yo gone buy somethin'?"

"Yeah, I'm thinking maybe your boss can help me with a present for my girlfriend."

"He can sho nuff do that, my man. You hang loose now." He walked back to the edge of the sidewalk, looking up and down the street. I was forgotten.

Inside the building activity was much as it had been the time before. The drones bent over their desks with headphones clasped over their ears talking into phone mikes were oblivious to my presence. At the end of the center aisle, I could see Coltrane behind the glass wall of his office. He was kneeling in front of the safe behind his desk. I walked quickly toward the office.

I'd forgotten about his door, though. When I pushed on it nothing happened. So, I knocked loudly to get his attention. He jumped upright and spun around. When he saw me, his face turned ashy and his eyes widened. I motioned for him to open the door.

He hesitated, looking from side to side, but the door in front of which I stood seemed to be the only way in or out of the office, and I made it clear by my expression that I wasn't going anywhere. Finally, he took the two steps to his desk and reached underneath it. The door swung open, and I entered.

As I approached him, Coltrane retreated behind his desk and sat down. Once he was seated some of his old smugness returned. The king was on his throne, so all must be right in his kingdom. I sat in the chair in front of his desk, leaning forward with my forearms resting on my thighs. I just stared at him until I noticed a slight twitching in his cheeks just below his eyes. Maybe all was *not* so right in his kingdom.

"W-what you d-doin' here, Pennyback? We both know you ain't got no intention of buyin' nothin' from me."

I continued to stare at him, letting him stew for a while. Then, I leaned forward, causing him to lean away from me. While he was thus distracted, I reached under the rim of the chair seat and retrieved the bug, palming it in my left hand.

"You're right," I said. "I'm not here to buy anything from you. Actually, I'm here to give you the chance to save your miserable hide."

"What the fuck you talkin' 'bout?" He looked genuinely puzzled. "You threatenin' me or somethin'?

Was I? I suppose I was. Of course, I wouldn't have put it quite so bluntly.

"Let's just say that your current lines of endeavor, if continued, could be hazardous to your health," I said. "For instance, your efforts to take merge street gangs and move into the African community are not wise, and I strongly recommend you rethink that particular operation."

His eyes got all round and goggly, and his lip quivered. "I don't know what you talkin' 'bout. All I want to do with my African brothers is invest a little bread and help them get rich."

I had to give the guy credit. He was almost good enough to lie to me and pull it off. But, the flickering of his eyes gave him away. At that moment I knew he'd been pulling a major scam. He had no real desire to invest in anything – it was a way of diverting attention away from his real objective.

"I don't think so," I said. I slipped the bug into my jacket pocket. I imagine Blood was listening to the conversation with interest, unless the two devices recording simultaneously were interfering with each other. "I think you just wanted Joseph Nkrumah to *think* you were looking to get your hooks in the businesses up there, when what you were really after was making it the base of your new gang operation."

His Adam's apple bobbed up and down. I'd hit a nerve. He looked at me as if I'd grown an extra head.

"What gang operation? I ain't got no gang."

"You're certainly intending to have a gang," I said. "And, worse – you're willing to murder people to get it."

"Man, you crazy! I ain't kilt nobody."

That was technically true, but in the eyes of the law, if he'd ordered his man Wilson to kill someone, he was equally guilty. The fact that he issued said orders in the pursuit of a criminal enterprise only increased his culpability. All that's legal jargon for, this turd was as guilty as sin, and he was sitting there staring across his desk at me trying to convince me he wasn't. He wasn't doing a good job of it.

"Oh, I can believe that. I saw how you reacted when I popped your boy in the nose. You're not the type to get your hands dirty as long as you have shitheads like him around to do your messy work for you."

"You talkin' 'bout Billy? Naw, man, you got it wrong. Billy, he just don't like to see nobody dissin' me, you dig. He won't gone do nothin' but bust you up a little – teach you some manners. That was some smooth move you done put on him. Where you learn to fight like that?"

His con man habits were kicking in. He was trying to get me talking about myself, but, thanks to Blood's mini-course on con men I was on to him.

"Pardon me if I think you're full of bullshit. I think your boy Billy does a lot more than just bust people up. I think he's been killing taxi drivers under your orders."

"Now, why in hell I want to be killin' taxi drivers?" He began tapping his fingers on the edge of his desk, and beads of sweat popped out on his forehead.

I leaned forward and put my right hand on the desk, mimicking his tapping motion. Startled, he looked down at his hand, and then snatched it back, putting it in his lap.

"You know," I said. "I've been wondering myself why you would go to such extreme measures – especially, given your . . . uh . . . shall we say . . . aversion to blood and all. All I can come up with is you figured it would scare Nkrumah and his people and make them roll over. It hasn't worked, has it? What I can't figure is why would a con artist want to get mixed up in gang activity?"

"You just guessin'. You ain't got no proof, 'cause if you did the po-leece would be settin' there talkin' to me, or I'd be in the lock up."

He was partly right. I didn't have any proof that I could turn over to the authorities. But, he didn't know that.

"I might not have concrete proof, but I have enough circumstantial evidence to make your life pretty uncomfortable."

"But, you ain't gone to the cops yet. Why?"

"Because, first, I want you to turn off your moves on the immigrant community – leave them alone. You're right about me not having enough to pin the murders on you, but it's just a matter of time before the police get onto you. As far as I'm concerned, that's between you and them. I'm just looking out for my clients."

My aversion to lying doesn't extend to bad

guys. I can look a crook in the eye and lie my ass off without a twinge of guilt. He hadn't completely bought it, though. The set of his jaw told me he still thought he could bluff his way past it.

"Why I should be doin' anything for you? Don't sound like nothin' in it for me. 'Sides, you said *first* – that mean you want somethin' else, right?"

"Yes, there is one other thing," I said. "There's the matter of the diamonds."

"What diamonds?" His lips quivered and his eyes flicked right and left.

"Don't play dumb. You told me you could get me a deal on some diamonds, and I know you gave a one carat stone to your cousin."

"Oh, you mean them diamonds. What about 'em?"

"I want you to turn them over to me."

He leaned back in his chair and gave me a strange look. Then, he laughed.

"I see what you up to now. Hell, you ain't no better'n me. You don't give a fuck 'bout them Africans – you just want to gyp outa them stones. Well, fuck you. You ain't gettin' 'em."

"You should really reconsider that," I said.

"Have you ever asked yourself where those diamonds came from?"

"Don't matter. I ain't givin' 'em to you, and that's that."

Twenty-Five

He'd as much confessed to knowing about the cabbie murders, but it was still my word against his. I felt like lunging across the desk and smashing his face in.

I was tensing up to smack him when my phone rang. I pulled it out of my pocket and saw that it was Buster calling.

"Yeah, bro," I said. "I'm in the middle of something right now. Can I call you back?"

"This'll only take a minute, Al. It's about that shithead who attacked you this morning. The lab checked the knife he used, and they can't say a hundred percent, but it is the same type blade used in killing the cab drivers."

That got my attention. "Just how sure are they?"

"Shit," he said. "You know how these lab nerds can be. They never come right out and give you a yes or no answer. Guy said he's 'bout sixty percent sure Wilson's knife is the murder weapon. I briefed my boss, and he's going to the DA to see if they think we got enough for an indictment. He agreed it was enough for me to keep on with the case."

Coltrane was staring at me, and I knew he was wondering who was on the other end of the phone. Guys like him aren't comfortable being in situations they can't control.

"You get anything out of . . . shithead . . . yet?"

"Naw – he's still unconscious. Doc says he might have a concussion, so ain't no tellin' when I'll be able to question him."

"Let me know what you find out," I said, and broke the connection.

As I put my phone back into my pocket, I looked at Coltrane, raising my left eyebrow and cocking my head.

"What? Why you lookin' at me like that?"

Some people think a professional con man can't be conned. I'm not one of those people. If you find the right button to push, *anyone* can be manipulated. Coltrane had a lot of buttons – he couldn't stand the sight of blood for one thing, and he liked to think that by manipulating others from behind the screen, he was immune from the realities of the world he was mucking with. When it looked like that world was slipping behind the curtain with him, he got worried. The sweat on his knitted brow, and the way the muscles in his cheeks kept doing the tango told me that he was seeing glimpses of the world, and he didn't like it. I decided to push his 'fear' button one more time.

"That was my friend, Buster," I said. "You remember him, the police detective? Well, right now, he's talking to your man Wilson about why the knife he attacked me with this morning is the same blade used to kill seven cab drivers.

That button sent a jolt through his system. The muscles in his cheek switched from a tango to a mariachi, and his skin got all waxy and ashy looking, as if he'd been out in the cold without skin lotion. But, I wasn't done.

"You know, some of those drivers were working as couriers for an international diamond smuggling ring. Your boy made a big mistake taking those stones. The people they really belong to want them back, and I don't think they're in a mood to negotiate for them, if you know what I mean."

"I – I don't know what you talkin' 'bout," he said. But, there was a note of desperation in his voice. "Billy, he done brought me them diamonds, but he didn't tell me where they come from. If he done gone out and robbed and kilt somebody, it ain't my doin'."

"Come on, Coltrane. Billy Wilson doesn't break wind without your permission, and he doesn't have the brain cells to come up with this."

There's one drawback to using fear as a motivator. It reaches a point, like torture, where the victim is numb to it. I'd overestimated how far I needed to push Coltrane. He was scared – that much was plain in his expression – but, his innate greed won out. He was willing to play his con to the limit, gambling that I might be bluffing, or that his skill as a con man, which had served him so well for so long, would enable him to prevail yet again.

"You gone have to prove that, brother man," he said. "And, I be bettin' you ain't got no real proof. I give it to you, though, you got yourself a big pair of balls, tryin' to come in here and pull a scam on Deacon Coltrane. Man, I been doin' this since I was a kid on the streets conning the neighbor ladies out of change for ice cream. You gone have to wake up early in the mornin' to fool the Deacon, Jack. Now, why don't you get your ass outa my face – what you say, don't let the door hit you in the ass on the way out."

He laughed – weakly – but, still he laughed. He thought he had me. He didn't know, though. I still had one card left to play. It wasn't one I necessarily wanted to use, but he was leaving me no choice.

I got up and walked out of his office, down the center aisle with all the people on either side talking into phones trying to part a lot of poor fools from their money, out the door and around the corner of the building to my car. I got in and slammed the door.

I sat there for a while, staring at the dirty brick wall.

Finally, I pulled out my cell phone and phoned Blood.

"It's a go," I said when he answered.

Twenty-Six

After making the necessary phone calls, I just sat there in my car staring at the brick wall. There was no turning back.

The strange thing is - while I felt a pricking of annoyance at having to compromise my sense of right and wrong - having to cooperate with the dark side didn't make me feel guilty, and I should have. That bothered me.

There was, though, nothing to be done about it now. I turned the key in the ignition, and my Volkswagen's engine hummed faithfully. The heater began pumping warm air. I backed out of the parking slot, spun the wheel right and pressed the gas pedal. The Bug glided smoothly onto the street. The kid on sentry duty in front of the building smiled and nodded as I drove past.

Just before I reached the corner I glanced in my rearview mirror. A large black SUV was pulling to the curb in front of Coltrane's building. Four men in dark suits got out and headed for the entrance.

I turned the corner before I could see how the kid on sentry duty dealt with the new visitors.

Twenty-Seven

The rest of Thursday went by like many days do when we have no cases to work. Heather did whatever it is she does at the computer – mostly, I'm convinced, because she's a lot more comfortable communing with that silent machine and its blinking displays than she is with people. I sat in my office, alternating between looking out the window at the naked limbs of the trees that framed the blue-gray sky and the leaden blue waters of the ship channel, sandwiched between the shiny walls of the towering condos behind our building, and the walls with their paucity of decorations. For once, though, I passed on my masochistic exercise of playing chess against the computer.

At a quarter of five, I decided to call it a day. I don't really remember what I said to Heather as I breezed through the outer office, or if she responded. Nor do I remember much about the drive home, or what transpired after I arrived.

Sandra sensed that I was troubled, so, after a quiet supper of ham sandwiches and tossed salad, washed down with beer in my case, white wine in hers, she retired to the sofa and busied herself grading papers, while

I cleaned the kitchen. When I'd scoured the sink a third time until it was shining like new, I joined her on the sofa. She had the radio playing softly – big band tunes from the forties – so I just sat there with my head back on the cushions and let the music wash over me.

Around ten, we both decided it was time for sleep, and that's what we did. She kissed me lightly on the forehead and turned in bed with her back to me and the blanket pulled up until it almost covered her completely. I lay there for a long time watching her until the steady rise and fall of the blanket told me she'd drifted off to sleep. For a long time after that, I lay on my back with the blanket pulled up to my chin, staring up at the gray ceiling.

I don't remember falling asleep. The next thing I knew, I was awakened by the shifting of the bed as Sandra threw off the covers and got out. I rolled over and watched as she made a dash across the chilly floor to the bathroom. I waited until I heard the sound of the commode flushing to get up myself.

I padded to the window and pulled the curtains aside. The sky outside was gray and sad looking. It matched my mood.

I was still standing there when Sandra came out of the bathroom.

"Feel like running today?" she asked.

"No," I said without turning around. "Looks like rain. Maybe I'll pass today. What do you want for breakfast?"

"I'm not very hungry. Just toast and coffee, I think."

I turned around to find her standing a few feet away looking at me with a worried look on her face. She was good at picking up on my moods, but she seldom pushed. She would patiently wait until I was ready to talk about it.

"Sounds good to me," I said. "I'll fix us up as soon as I shower and dress."

She turned away and went to the closet to get dressed. I went into the bathroom.

Breakfast was quiet. It didn't take long to prepare, and even less time to eat. Cleaning up afterwards was quickly done – just two plates and two coffee cups. The leftover coffee could be rewarmed, so I just turned the coffee maker off.

Sandra was ready to leave for school before I'd finished my second cup of coffee, so she quietly kissed me on the cheek, said she'd see me at supper, and left. I sat at the kitchen table until the half-cup of coffee that I'd been staring at was too cold to drink. I poured it into the sink, rinsed out the cup, pulled on my jacket and headed for the office.

Heather is even better than Sandra at reading my mood. Of course, she's known me longer. She just nodded and smiled as I walked grumpily past her desk heading to my office. Inside the office, I shucked my jacket and slumped into my chair. I didn't even feel like looking out the window, and hardly noticed the wall. I was basically sitting there looking at nothing and feeling like shit.

Irritability is the best way of describing my feeling – the blinking of the damn red light on the phone pissed me off. I felt like snatching the instrument up and throwing it at the wall. Blinking red light! Oh yeah, I thought, Heather's calling me to let me know I have a call or a visitor. *"Get yourself together, Pennyback!"*

"Yeah, Heather," I said, trying to remove any trace of peevishness from my voice. "What is it?"

"Buster on the line for you, boss." There was tension in her voice. I had a lot of making up to do, with her *and* Sandra.

"Okay, thanks, honey bunch. Put him through."

"You got it, boss." She was a little chirrupy sounding that time. So, she wasn't totally pissed at me.

"Hello, Buster," I said when she

transferred him. "What's up?"

"I got a whole bunch of news for you pardner, way too much for the phone," he said. "You want to meet me at Mom's and we can talk?"

He sounded positively giddy. It aroused my curiosity. If there's anything that will yank me out of a blue mood it's a puzzle, and his sudden change from the angry cop being disrespected by the chain of command to – well – this, touched that part of my brain that takes over when there's a riddle to solve.

"Okay, meet you there in an hour?"

He rang off. I was betting he'd be there and chin deep in biscuits and gravy by the time I arrived. I put my jacket on, and stopped at Heather's desk on my way out.

She looked up at me, a half smile on her elfin face. "You feeling better now?"

That was all. No, 'what's up with you?' or anything like that. She knew I'd tell her when, and if, I felt like it.

"Yeah," I said. "The thought of Mom's food always makes me feel better."

She made a sniffing sound, and wrinkled her nose. "The thought of what she puts in that food makes me feel like I should visit my doctor. I don't see how you and Buster can stuff yourselves with so much fat."

"Fat's what gives it flavor," I said defensively.

I wasn't quite happy, but I felt like I might be getting there. I was still debating it when I parked a half block from Mom's, walked through the chilly air and into her place, where I was hit with a warm blast from the kitchen. I'd been right, too. Buster was already there, attacking a large steak and a Mount Olympus-like mound of scrambled eggs in one plate, and a three-stack of pancakes with a stack of bacon slices and four biscuits in the other. Next to his elbow was a large white ceramic mug of coffee with so much milk in it, it looked more like dirty milk than coffee, and a quart-sized glass of orange juice.

The smell of hot grease hung in the air like a wool blanket. Mom perched on her customary stool in front of the door, her large brown arm resting on the cash register. Today, she didn't have her usual head cloth. Her hair, black with strings of white showing, was straightened and slick, reflecting glints of the overhead lights. She smiled that open-mouth, gap-toothed smile of hers when she saw me.

"Hey, hon," she said, her southern accent thick and syrupy. "You gone have what yo friend havin?"

"No, just pancakes, bacon and hash browns for me," I said. "With black coffee and a regular-sized glass of grapefruit juice."

"You just go on and set yourself down. I'll have yo food out directly."

When Mom said directly, she meant the food would arrive almost as soon as your butt started warming the chair. The cook, who I had heard was also her husband – number five –, was one of the fastest in town. Of course, when you fry just about everything, it doesn't take long.

Buster glanced up at me as I took my chair facing the front, but was too busy chewing to do anything but nod and make a sound like, 'hmmph gnn!'

I sat quietly and let him finish chewing. He washed it down with a long swig of orange juice.

"You know, it's not good for you, washing your food down like that," I said. "I read somewhere that it keeps the digestive secretions from working properly."

"Shit, it all goes the same place. I ain't had no problems yet."

"Just saying. Now, what was it you had to tell me?"

He put his knife and fork down, took a sip of coffee, and leaned forward, his elbows on the table. Mom came up with my food, and after putting it down, slapped at his elbows.

"Didn't yo ma ever teach you not to put yo elbows on the table when you eatin', boy?"

"Yessum," Buster said, ducking his head like a kid who has just been scolded by his mother. "Sorry." He put his hands on his lap.

Mom patted his bald head and waddled away. I laughed quietly.

"Ssh," he said quietly. "She hear you, she might come back."

"Okay, what's so important you yank me away from important work?"

"Important work, my ass. I know you ain't got nothin' to do right now." He laughed. "Anyway, I wanted to let you know we got Billy Wilson dead to rights on the cab driver murders. They found his Pontiac about six blocks from your office, and guess what – he had plastic gloves and some kind of plastic blouse things you wear over your jacket in the trunk. And, the lab guys found a smidgen of blood on the hinge of his switchblade that they matched to Dudu Nkomo. Seems he didn't clean it as good as he thought."

"I guess that pretty much means the DA will go for an indictment."

"Bet your sweet ass. Old Billy done woke up late last night. I went over and hit him 'tween the eyes with what we found. First, he tried to play all innocent, but when I told him 'bout the blood on his knife, he caved in like a sand castle at Ocean City when the tide comes in. Started singin' like a church choir. Too bad the District don't have the death penalty, 'cause if it did, that dumb fuck would be takin' the big sleep for sure. He'll never see the streets again, though, and that's at least somethin'."

"This'll put Coltrane out of business too, I imagine. Wilson wouldn't have done this on his own."

"Oh yeah, he dropped a dime on the Deacon all right," Buster said. "Only thing is, old Deacon ain't gone have his day in court."

"Why the hell not?"

I knew what the answer would be before he said it, but kept my face impassive.

"Turns out, you was right. Some of the cabbies were working with this diamond smuggling ring. They picked up the rocks at National Airport and delivered them to contacts here. When Wilson was rifling through the glove compartment to get rid of the trip ticket, he stumbled across 'em. Took 'em home to the boss. He said he got four packages of diamonds – didn't know how many, but said his cut when his boss fenced 'em would be fifty grand. Anyway, seems the smugglers found out what happened. They paid Deacon a visit yesterday."

"I take it their visit wasn't a friendly one?"

"You could say that," he said. "They cut off one of his pinky fingers. That must have made him open that safe behind his desk, 'cause when we got there, it was open and empty. Old Deacon, minus one pinky was sittin' on the floor next to the safe with a .9mm slug in his forehead."

"Shit," I said. "Someone did this in broad daylight and got away?"

"No, not exactly. One of the phone operators was on the way to take a piss and saw these four dudes arguing with Deacon. He sneaked out and called 911. By the time we got there, though, the feds had already arrived and caught the four dudes as they were coming out the front. They nabbed 'em before they knew what was happenin'. Had four bags of diamonds on 'em. When we went inside, we found Deacon. 'Course, the feds want to prosecute 'em on the smuggling charge, but the dude in charge, agent name of Ted Striker, said he'd talk to the U.S. Attorney 'bout including the murder charge, and see if they can get the case moved to Virginia where they got the death penalty."

That lifted some of the blackness from my thoughts. At least the smugglers would be brought to justice.

"So, you solved the taxi driver murders, and the feds got their smugglers. I guess everyone's happy."

"Well, not everybody," he said. "That asshole Helsing's chewin' nails right now. Me bein' right 'bout the murders made him look stupid, and with the feds creditin' me for helpin' 'em with the smuggling case and all, his star's a little tarnished down at the department. Word is, they be movin' him from the street crime task force and back to public relations or community outreach."

"Guess that makes you a hero," I said. "Think you'll get a promotion out of it?"

He certainly deserved to get something for it. He'd stuck to his guns when the weight of the bureaucracy was against him – lived up to the police motto, 'to serve and protect' while a self-serving bureaucrat like Helsing was following the path of least resistance.

"I didn't do anything, bro." He took another sip of coffee. "If you hadn't kicked over a few rocks, I'd still be bustin' my head against a stone wall. You the one that deserves a medal.

I didn't feel like I deserved a medal. I'd as

good as killed Coltrane. Oh sure, I hadn't pulled the trigger that put a lead slug in his head, but I'd been the one who sent the men there who did. That, though, was something I could never tell Buster. While he might understand – we'd been friends too long for him to do otherwise – but it would change our relationship if he knew. I didn't feel any sorrow about him dying; just about having been an instrument in his death. Even a slug like him deserved due process, and I'd short-circuited that process. I frowned down at my coffee cup.

"What you lookin' so sad about, bro?" he asked. "We done cleaned up a bit of the dirt off the city streets. You oughta be feelin' good 'bout that."

"Yeah, but people died. I mean, Coltrane was bad – no doubt about it – but, he should have had his day in court."

I hadn't noticed Mom come up to our table. For a big woman, she can move as quietly as a cat stalking a bird. "Y'all talkin' 'bout that fella Deacon Coltrane? The one what got hisself kilt yestiddy over in Anacostia?"

"Yeah, that's him," Buster said. "You know him?"

"I know of him. He been runnin' rackets over there for years – takin' money from anybody stupid enough to buy that junk he be sellin'. You ask me, I say good riddance."

"Mom, it ain't Christian to talk like that 'bout the dead," Buster said, but there was no reproach in his tone.

"I think the Lawd'll forgive me for not bein' sorry that man dead. He ain't done nothin' but corrupt the young people in our community, with his loan sharkin', and turnin' young girls out on the streets. Ain't a racket in the projects he didn't have his grubby hands in."

I realized that I probably should have consulted Mom from the start. She was the doyen of Washington's working class community, having been in the city for as long as most people could remember. She knew everything and everyone. If she said Coltrane was dirty, there was a better than even chance he was dirty. I was curious, though, about the newspaper reports of his beneficence.

"According to the newspaper reports," I said. "Coltrane was a pillar of the community. All I could find were stories about his charitable donations."

She made a rude sound through her wide nose. "What them white folk what work at the newspaper know 'bout anything? They come down here and take pictures of some fool givin' a check to some other fool, or cuttin' a ribbon, and they go back and write they stories. Us who live down here see a different picture. Deacon Coltrane ain't never give nobody nothin' he didn't 'spect repayment for with interest. He pay for buildin' a shelter for women get beat by they husbands, you can bet he be havin' half the women in that shelter turnin' tricks for him within a week it open. Ever body in the place be on his payroll, so they don't never tell the law." She glared at Buster. "And the po-leece, they don't come down here lessen they gone 'rest somebody or bust some po niggah's head."

"But, with all that publicity, he'll probably have a pretty big funeral. Everyone can't think he's bad." I was fishing, but Mom wasn't biting.

"Only people gone be goin' to Deacon's funeral be pimps, hos and hustlers. Ain't no decent people gone be wastin' they time, lessen they wants to make sure he really dead. The man was bad, I tell you – as bad as they come."

"How come you know so much 'bout his illegal activity and the police never did?"

"Aw, come on, boy," she said. "You know well as I do, folks in this part of town don't talk to no po-leece, not even a colored man like you. The po-leece ain't give them no reason to trust 'em. They just do what they have to do to survive. 'Sides, it ain't healthy for a colored person to be too friendly with you po-leece."

"You're friendly enough with Buster here," I said.

"Ain't nobody gone bother with me, and 'sides, this boy here, I just don't think of him as po-leece. He just a bad mannered boy what like to come here and stuff his face – can't help he done took the wrong profession."

With that, she waddled off to tend to other customers.

"Damn," Buster said. "We got to do a better job of reachin' out to the people in this city, that's fo sure. Hey, before I forget, Wilson also spilled everything he knew 'bout Coltrane's plan to merge the street gangs. Man, that brother dreamed big. He was talkin' to every gang in the city, from the black drug dealers to the Asians to the Hispanics. He was gonna split the city up into sections, with each of 'em havin' complete control of their section, with him sittin' at the top of the pyramid controllin' things. Said it was to cut down on inter-gang squabbles and be more efficient."

"Pretty ambitious for a petty con man."

"Yeah, and if he hadn't overreached by killin' those cab drivers, he might have pulled it off. Man, can you imagine how hard it would be to police this town if all the gangs got together. It'd be like Chicago back when the mob controlled things."

I could imagine it. In a city where a large percentage of the population didn't trust the police, having a major criminal enterprise embedded throughout the neighborhoods would have been a nightmare. Leaving things as they were was bad enough, but I could see Buster's point. Going after the individual gangs was the best of a bunch of bad choices.

"So, you'll keep chipping away at the street gangs, I guess. It seems like trying to keep your fingers in the dyke, but the ocean keeps crashing through somewhere else."

He held up his fingers, waggling them at me. "Better than havin' the whole damn ocean trying to crash through where you got your fingers, though."

Twenty-Eight

Saturday morning dawned bright, with a cloudless blue sky and temperatures hovering in the mid-forties. By the time I got home, Mom's words had sunk in, and I wasn't feeling quite so guilty. Sandra picked up on my lighter mood.

We'd cooked supper together the night before. A combination of my down home oriented chili with cornbread and lots of peppers and her healthier tossed salad with goat cheese and olive oil with pine nuts sprinkled on. The salad was actually good – good enough for me to ask for seconds. I think it was the pine nuts. She reciprocated by eating half of a second bowl of chili, even though the jalapenos I'd put in it caused her eyes to water and her face got all red.

After cleaning up, we decided to retire to the bedroom – it was a very active retirement, and for a change, I slept soundly and without dreams.

I rolled off the bed and walked to the window. Looking down at the backyard, I saw a small herd of white tail deer grazing at the edge of the woods. The leader, a ten-point buck, grazed, but every few minutes he'd raise his head and scan three-sixty. Seeing no danger, he resumed feeding.

I wasn't aware Sandra had gotten out of bed until I felt the warmth from her body and the softness of her breasts pressing into my back.

"Feel like a good brisk run this morning?" she asked.

I circled slowly until the pressure of her breasts was against my chest. "I *feel* a lot of things," I said. "But, I suppose a quick jog through the forest would be good for both of us."

We got into our sweats, complete with knit caps pulled down over our ears. The temperature felt only slightly chilly, and you might feel warm when running, but if you're not careful, you can get a case of hypothermia in forty degree weather or damage to exposed skin. The tops of the ears seem to be especially susceptible to both heat and cold.

They say that you can check your conditioning by talking as you run. If you find it difficult to do, your lungs are out of shape. Thing is, I don't like talking when I run. That's my time for thinking and soaking up my surroundings. I'm a Zen runner. Once I get my stride going and my breathing steady, I'm into the zone. Sandra was the same. She'd get that elbow swing just right, her long legs stretching out in front of her reaching for the ground, her eyes on a spot twenty yards in front of her, and you could tell she was there – in her zone.

It's not that when we ran we weren't aware of each other. I know I was acutely aware of her. Of the way her hip muscles rippled as she ran, and the way her breasts bounced. I'd like to think she was admiring my fine male physique as well.

But, it wasn't just her that I was aware of. When I ran, just like when I meditated, I was *aware*. I saw all the colors – the blue of the sky, the green of the vegetation, and the flashes of color of the birds that scattered squawking as we approached their perches. I could feel the gentle caress of the air sliding over my skin, or the occasional brush of a bush or plant at the side of the trail. I heard the sound of my breathing, the dull thud of my feet on the soft earth, birds with their cacophony of calls, and the chittering of squirrels chasing each other through the trees as they took advantage of the warmth to gather more nuts or just frolic in the sun. I smelled the rich, heady aroma of the earth, stirred up by our passing.

Most of all, though, I was able to think. I could let my mind run free. Not rampant, like a leaf in the wind buffeted to and fro at the whims of the air currents, but at the same time, not on iron rails unable to veer from its charted course. No, it was the type of freedom that allowed me to venture down one avenue of thought, while at the same time keeping an eye on paths that ran off in all other directions. I could *see* all around me. Find the loose threads that only had to be picked up to be traced back to their logical origins.

As I ran – a loose, loping jog – breathing easily through my nose and watching the wispy vapor as my warm breath met the cool morning air, I was following a particular path. It was a path with many forks and divergences, with dozens of loose threads that all seemed to end up back at the same starting point.

One thread was one that led me through a consideration of the crime situation in the District, in particular, that part of the District known as Anacostia. The District's Southeast quadrant, bisected from northeast to southwest by the Anacostia River, in the late 1990s accounted for over half of the city's violent crimes, including over 400 murders per year, 60 percent of which were never solved. The police force, copying New York City, had a zero tolerance policy, but instead of driving crime rates down, it only made it more difficult for the 4,500 cops like Buster to solve crimes. People in the poor neighborhoods like Anacostia not only didn't trust the police, they actively disliked them.

That thread led to Coltrane.

This situation gave people like Delmar Coltrane a pretty free hand to do just about what they pleased. He'd been able to operate below the official radar - although what he did was known by his victims and other residents – running his rackets while appearing to the public outside the projects as the generous black businessman who was respected by the people. That thread had been amorphous, twisting in and out and around so many obstacles, it had confused me at first.

Another thread was Washington's demographics. A predominantly black city, immigration from Asia, Latin America, and Africa during the 90s had introduced a number of ethnically diverse communities into what were in fact separate cities – black in the Northeast, Southwest, and much of the Southeast, mostly white in the affluent Northwest. The immigrants had spread out through the city depending upon their economic situation, with the poorer ones carving out little enclaves in the predominantly black neighborhoods. Language and customs, and a distrust of authority brought with them from their home countries, made them vulnerable – mainly to street gangs made up of members of their own ethnic groups. This thread, too, eventually led me to Coltrane, whose greed and ego had convinced him that he could take advantage of the situation and make himself the city's crime czar, sitting at the top of a pyramid of criminal activity covering the area.

The final thread, the one I really didn't want to follow, but had no choice but to pick up and track to its origin – or destination – was that one that pertained to my own actions. I wasn't mourning Coltrane's death. He deserved to die. I had in my lifetime dispatched not a few people like him. But, in the other cases, I'd done it myself, not used a surrogate. My mind was wrestling with that. Had I cooperated with van Klerk and Arens because I was afraid I'd be unable to bring Coltrane down through my own efforts? Or, had it been in retaliation for the arrogance he displayed at out last meeting? I could always tell myself that I had no way of knowing that the two smugglers, in the process of retrieving their merchandise, would kill Coltrane. But, I knew that line of reasoning was bullshit. There was no way they could leave him alive. The fact was - if they suspected I knew who they really were, they'd probably would have come after me. Might have anyway if they hadn't been swept up by the feds coming out of a murder scene. I think Blood knew all this when he came up with the plan in the first place. In the back of my mind, I think I knew it as well.

I had put in an escape route, if only Coltrane's greed and ego had allowed him to take it. He'd been king of the hill in the ghetto for so long, I think he thought himself invulnerable. He'd had a hand in his own fate. I was just the instrument bringing it about – one in a number of instruments.

Over all these tangled threads, though, hovered a number of facts. Joseph Nkrumah's community was no longer under siege. The murders of seven cab drivers would be avenged – in Coltrane's case, had already been avenged. The city of Washington, with all the problems it had to face, was spared having to deal with a well-organized, city-wide criminal enterprise, and, finally, an international smuggling cartel had been dismantled. Arens and van Klerk, along with two of their confederates, wasted no time in making deals with the authorities in their effort to reduce their possible sentences – including trying to get the venue of their trial moved back to the District where the death penalty for Coltrane's murder wouldn't be on the table. Arrest warrants and requests for extradition were zipping across the Atlantic while Sandra and I did our morning jog.

The greater good. That was what it was all about. Sometimes, in order to serve the greater good, you have to be a little bad.

The last stretch of trail before reaching the backyard was through a thick stand of evergreens and black gum trees. The limbs of the taller evergreens interlaced over the trail putting much of it in shadow. It was like running through a tunnel. The bright light of the morning sun hit me in the face like a physical blow as we came out of the trees. I'd passed Sandra, and with long, loping strides, I aimed for the back porch. I could hear the dull thud of her footsteps behind me as she pumped her legs to catch up. A grazing herd of young white tail deer, spooked at our sudden appearance, made barking noises and bound off toward the trees to the west.

Sandra caught up, and we arrived at the back steps in a photo finish, both only slightly winded.

"That felt good," she said.

"Yes, it did," I said. "Feel like a workout in the barn?"

She flexed her biceps. "You sure you feel like having your butt kicked?"

I took a step back and went into the horse stance. Four quick alternating punches, each accompanied by a sharp 'Ya!', a forward snap kick with my left foot, and then I jumped straight up in the air, spinning to the right, kicking out with my right foot as I came back around, 'Ai-ya!', and landing balanced on my left foot, my right foot only inches from her face. "That look to you like I might get my butt k

I had to give her credit. She neither blinked nor flinched. Just looked levelly at me with those icy blue eyes of hers, a half smile on her face. "Not bad," she said. "Let's go see how you do when you're not kicking air."

"You're on."

We headed for the barn. She walked along, her shoulder brushing lightly against mine.

"This was a tough case, wasn't it?" she asked.

"One of my toughest," I said. "Some hard decisions had to be made."

"Were they made for the right reasons?" She stopped and laid a hand on my forearm, looking deep into my eyes.

"I think they were."

"And, in the end, were the innocent protected, and the guilty punished?"

"Definitely."

She shrugged. There was no need for her to say anything. It was all there in her expression.

Other books by this author:

Al Pennyback mysteries

Color Me Dead
Memorial to the Dead
Deadline
Dead, White, and Blue
A Good Day to Die
The Day the Music Died
Die, Sinner
Deadly Intentions
Death by Design
Till Death Do Us Part
Deadly Dose
Dead Man's Cove
Dead Men Don't Answer
Deadly Paradise
Kiss of Death
Death in White Satin
Death and Taxis

The Buffalo Soldier series:

Buffalo Soldier: Trial by Fire
Buffalo Soldier: Homecoming
Buffalo Soldier: Incident at Cactus Junction
Buffalo Soldier: Peacekeepers
Buffalo Soldier: Renegade
Buffalo Soldier: Escort Duty
Buffalo Soldier: Yosemite

Other fiction

Angel on His Shoulder
She's No Angel
Child of the Flame
Pip's Revenge
Wallace in Underland
Further Adventures of Wallace in Underland
Dead Letter and Other Tales
The White Dragons
The Dragon's Lair
The Last Gunfighters
The Culling

Nonfiction

Things I Learned from My Grandmother About Leadership and Life
Taking Charge: Effective Leadership for the Twenty-first Century
Grab the Brass ring
African Places: A Photographic Journey Through Zimbabwe and southern Africa

About the Author

Charles Ray has been writing fiction since his teens. He won a Sunday school magazine writing contest when he was thirteen, and having his byline on a short story published in a national publication forever hooked him on writing. During his time in the army (1962-1982) he often moonlighted as a newspaper or magazine journalist, and was the editorial cartoonist for the Spring Lake (NC) News, a weekly newspaper, during the 1970s. In addition to his writing, he was an artist/cartoonist and photographer for a number of publications, including Ebony, Eagle and Swan, and Essence, and had a monthly cartoon feature and did several covers for Buffalo, a now-defunct magazine that was dedicated to showcasing the contributions of African-Americans to the country's military history.

After retiring from the army, he joined the U.S. Foreign Service, and served as a diplomat in posts in Asia and Africa until his retirement in 2012. He has worked and traveled throughout the world (Antarctica is the only continent he hasn't visited), and now, as a full time writer, continues to globetrot looking for interesting things to write about, draw, or take pictures of.

A native of Texas, he now calls Maryland home. For more on his writing and other projects, check one of the following Web sites:

http://redroom.com/member/charles-a-ray
http://charlesaray.blogspot.com
http://charlieray45.wordpress.com
http://www.twitter.com/charlieray45
http://www.facebook.com/charlieray45
http://www.flickr.com/photos/charlesray45/
http://www.viewbug.com/member/charlesray

Photo by Denise Ray-Wickersham

www.ingramcontent.com/pod-product-compliance
Lightning Source LLC
Chambersburg PA
CBHW071458170626
46811CB00007B/2623